TRANSITION AGE

An age shaped by systems. A generation shaped by their limits.

A world where history exists in a permanent artificial twilight.

TYLER CORRIVEAU

1st Edition, 2026
Paperback ISBN: 979-8-9946284-0-9
Hardcover ISBN: 979-8-9946284-3-0
eBook ISBN: 979-8-9946284-9-2

TRANSITION AGE
TRILOGY

TRANSITION AGE
BOOK 01

HORIZON FAULT
BOOK 02

THE UNCOUNTED
BOOK 03

Learn more at: transitionagetrilogy.com
Follow the series: @transitionagetrilogy

Dedicated to those who imagine other worlds and live on the edges of the systems that shape us.

Contents

The Precedent
Events Leading To The Transition Age

The Transition Age did not begin quietly. It was declared, ratified, and widely supported in the aftermath of global collapse.

After nearly a century of war, economic, and environmental devastation, the world as we knew it could no longer continue.

The collapse that preceded the Transition Age was not a singular turning point, but a sequence of events driven by self-serving imperialism in pursuit of sovereign survival and false democracy.

Public perception of global powers eroded as populations and international corporations could no longer trust their decisions.

This marked an unprecedented moment of global consensus to usher in a new era and world order, not born from optimism but of the necessity of survival.

What follows is not a complete history, but a record of the crises, escalations, and outcomes that made the Transition Age possible, and ultimately inevitable.

Pre-Transition Age: 2028 - 2092

2028: The ISS Deorbit Crisis

On August 5, 2028, years before the International Space Station was scheduled for controlled decommissioning, catastrophic system failures caused it to enter an uncontrolled deorbit. Without control over the surviving modules during atmospheric re-entry, the station crashed into Mexico City, resulting in widespread civilian casualties.

Multiple high-density districts were affected, causing structural damage and industrial contamination. In response to its international and orbital safety obligations, the United States and privatized aerospace conglomerates offer immediate assistance and recovery support.

Mexico, in response, swiftly denied any access and entry into the country, citing its national sovereignty and security concerns. Mexican authorities and influential cartel militias secured the impact zones, assuming control of the recoverable ISS wreckage. In the weeks following the impact, national intelligence leaks emerged, suggesting that several classified biotechnologies and Quantum AI chipsets may have survived reentry. Despite Mexican and U.S. officials denying the existence and nature of these technologies, increasing pressure from targeted inquiries and public discourse intensified the situation.

2029: The Siege of Mexico City

On June 29, 2029, after prolonged diplomatic failures concerning the ISS wreckage and escalating tensions along the U.S.–Mexico border, the United States launched a covert tactical operation. U.S. operatives orchestrate coordinated false-flag events in Tijuana and Monterrey to destabilize regional control and divert Mexican authorities and cartel militias from Mexico City. As infrastructure collapses and civilian unrest spreads, U.S. military forces execute amphibious landings along the Pacific coast near Acapulco. Within days, U.S. forces secure Mexico City and the ISS impact zones. Formal actions commence to suspend and dismantle Mexico's federal governance, transferring authority to U.S.-backed militarized control.

In response to international scrutiny, the U.S. frames the operation as a justified means to retrieve the ISS wreckage, secure the borders, and mitigate cartel violence. However, intelligence leaks in subsequent months suggest the invasion was premeditated. Theories emerge alleging that the true motives were the acquisition of rare mineral resources and oil reserves. Whistleblowers present evidence indicating that the ISS's deorbit was intentional, a deliberate act to justify the United States' territorial entry and control.

2032: The U.S. Energy Saturation

After a decade of reshoring manufacturing, accelerating AI data center expansion, and driving infrastructure electrification, the long-term impacts on the U.S. national grid reach a critical juncture. By 2032, rolling outages across states and multi-day blackouts in major cities became commonplace. As the crisis worsens and the energy capacity shortage begins to affect the economy, conflict arises among disjointed federal agencies trying to address the same problem.

The Department of Energy focuses its efforts on constructing the world's first city-scale fusion reactor, building on the success of smaller fusion systems deployed in data centers. Meanwhile, the Department of Defense pursues planning territorial expansion in Central and South America to secure control over oil reserves and offshore drilling claims. Inter-departmental conflicts intensify as they disagree on the viability of the plans and the decision to continue military escalation south of the border. While seeking congressional approvals, long-term risk projections and environmental consequences are classified, deferred, or excluded from formal assessments.

2033: The South American Missile Crisis

In 2033, federal efforts to de-escalate regional instability faltered due to competing agency agendas and fractured command authority. On April 16, 2033, AI-guided missile systems authorized for targeted strikes on remaining Mexican cartel and military installations malfunctioned mid-operation. Consequently, these strikes self-reroute, causing civilian casualties in major population centers across Central and South America. As global attention shifts to the unfolding disaster, internal power struggles within the U.S. government intensify. Rival federal factions covertly authorize additional missile strikes, presenting them as containment measures while deliberately destabilizing regional governments.

These actions aim to fracture local leadership, secure leverage over energy-rich territories, and consolidate strategic advantage amidst the ongoing energy crisis. The strikes trigger widespread retaliation and systemic political collapse throughout Central and South America. Escalation accelerates beyond diplomatic containment, drawing multiple nations into a prolonged continental conflict. What initially starts as a systematic failure becomes a defining inflection point in the destabilization of nation-states.

2041: The Great U.S. Occupation

By 2041, the United States had gained direct control over significant portions of Central and South America. These vast territories are no longer under military occupation or transitional governance but are instead placed under federal ownership. Political autonomy is stripped away, and these regions are administered through emerging privatized military structures.

The controlled territories remain economically crippled and environmentally unstable due to years of sustained conflict and infrastructure collapse. Widespread displacement persists among local populations, while early international relief efforts prioritize logistics, resource security, and geopolitical positioning over long-term humanitarian recovery.

That same year, a pivotal moment occurred in U.S. energy infrastructure. On September 9, 2041, the nation's first city-scale fusion reactor was successfully brought online in Virginia. This reactor supplied power to the Washington, D.C., metropolitan region and to national AI supercomputing systems. Federal plans are formally announced to expand fusion capacity across all U.S. states and territories.

In parallel, the U.S. government introduces redevelopment frameworks for climate-threatened and war-devastated regions. These frameworks outline vertical urban centers powered by fusion energy and are presented internationally as a blueprint for post-war recovery and climate resilience.

2058: The Prototype Vertical Age

By 2058, the accelerating rise in sea levels compels global urban restructuring, shifting from long-term planning to active implementation. Coastal erosion, flooding, and the failure of systemic infrastructure render significant portions of existing cities uninhabitable. Consequently, several low-lying metropolitan regions are formally abandoned, with cities including Miami and New Orleans becoming early symbols of irreversible environmental loss. In response, governments and corporate partners advance large-scale coastal reshaping initiatives, including the construction of artificial landmasses, vertical seawalls, and elevated megastructures intended to consolidate populations into dense, defensible regions. Along the Gulf and Pacific coasts of Mexico, as well as within former metropolitan centers across Central and South America, the first fully realized vertical megaregions began phased operation under federal and corporate oversight.

These early megacities span multiple former urban areas and introduce layered city design at an unprecedented scale. Structures rise to heights approaching one mile, integrating housing, industry, transportation, and governance into unified vertical systems. Prototype megaregions emerge in and around Mexico City, the Panama Canal Zone, São Paulo, Rio de Janeiro, Buenos Aires, and Santiago, transforming previously destabilized territories into controlled urban corridors.

2079: The Age of Limitless Energy

By 2079, every U.S. state and territory had at least one fusion reactor, providing a nationwide surplus of stable power and centralized infrastructure. This progress accelerated large-scale population relocation, encouraging and compelling residents from rural areas and declining municipalities to move into newly established megaregions across Central and South America. As these vertical cities come online, they are presented as centers of opportunity and stability, while the dissolution of local communities goes unnoticed.

The abundance of energy revolutionizes innovation across all sectors. AI-assisted research accelerates at unprecedented speeds, removing previous constraints on computation, manufacturing, and experimentation. Quantum-assisted systems are integrated into global communication networks, logistics, and governance, while medical infrastructure shifts from disease treatment to optimization and predictive intervention. Rapid progress follows in biotechnology, genetic engineering, neural interface development, and human longevity research. The line between biological and synthetic intelligence becomes increasingly blurred. As these capabilities expand, competition intensifies amongst governments, corporations, and research coalitions to secure dominance in artificial intelligence, robotics, biotechnology, and neurological systems. Regulatory frameworks lag behind deployment, creating conditions for systemic ethical erosion and subsequent conflict.

2082: World War III

On April 20, 2082, coordinated cyberterrorist networks operating out of Russia infiltrated fusion reactor control systems across multiple regions. They exploited vulnerabilities in the newly centralized energy infrastructure, triggering cascading failures in several city-scale fusion plants. Reactors malfunctioned and detonated in Washington, D.C., the Ashburn, Virginia data corridor, and multiple megacities across U.S.-controlled Central and South American territories. The Ashburn detonation caused a global connectivity crisis within minutes, destroying critical internet exchange points, hyperscale data centers, and AI compute infrastructure. These attacks were intended for systemic collapse while simultaneously disrupting power generation, data routing, financial markets, medical systems, U.S. artificial intelligence arms, and national communications networks. As a result, global markets froze, and AI-managed logistics, healthcare, finance, and autonomous operations failed, entering uncontrolled states.

In the aftermath, Russian military operations expanded across contested regions as U.S. forces, overwhelmed by internal devastation and loss of operational capacity, withdrew from Central and South America. Evacuation corridors were limited or suspended, leaving large civilian populations previously encouraged to relocate into these regions without federal protection or recovery support. This retreat ended U.S. territorial control in the region and marked a decisive turning point in the conflict. Vast areas of Central and South America became uninhabitable, while prolonged lockdowns and decontamination protocols surrounded Washington, D.C., as authorities struggled to contain radiation exposure, population displacement, and civil unrest.

2087: The Collapse of Nation-States

World War III officially concluded on November 5, 2087, leaving both the United States and Russia economically and politically drained. Five years of military escalation, unchecked spending, and failed bioweapon and artificial intelligence arms races have left both governments financially insolvent and structurally unstable. Consequently, localized governments erode across multiple regions as rebuilding efforts stall and public institutions crumble.

The sheer scale of civilian casualties, coupled with vast uninhabitable zones spanning multiple continents, has sparked unprecedented global outrage. Survivors, displaced populations, and international advocacy coalitions demand accountability for the decisions that led to continental devastation. Legal actions and formal inquiries are initiated through international bodies, while parallel uprisings within Russia accelerate the erosion of public trust in national governance.

By the end of the decade, the legitimacy of all sovereign governments is widely regarded as irreparably compromised. Movements advocating for the dismantling of traditional nation-states, dictatorships, and parliamentary systems gain global traction. Across multiple continents, populations are calling for the establishment of a centralized authority capable of preventing future large-scale annihilation and paving the way for the emergence of a unified global order.

Transition Age: 2093 - Present

2093: The United Federal Nations (UFN)

On October 24, 2093, the United Nations was formally reconstituted as the United Federal Nations, designated as the UFN. The reformation established a centralized global governing authority following the collapse of major world powers and sustained international demand for stability after World War III. The UFN is introduced as a permanent institution tasked with preventing future global conflict, regulating shared resources, and overseeing large-scale reconstruction.

Among its initial actions, the UFN established a single global currency called Global Credits and initiated the dissolution of national militaries. Enforcement authority is transferred to unified global security frameworks operating directly under UFN oversight. These measures are presented as essential steps to eliminate unilateral military action and ensure consistent global compliance.

In parallel, the UFN authorizes unprecedented corporate consolidation as a cornerstone of its recovery policy. Major corporations across various sectors, including consumer electronics, semiconductor manufacturing, artificial intelligence, global media, biotechnology, pharmaceuticals, and healthcare systems, are approved to merge into a limited number of dominant entities. These megacorporations are contractually obligated to finance and direct global reconstruction efforts, paving the way for a future characterized by efficiency, stability, and integrated governance under centralized oversight.

2094: The Formation of Horizon

On June 26, 2094, under the authority of the United Federal Nations, Horizon was officially established through the sanctioned merger of the world's largest consumer technology, semiconductor manufacturing, artificial intelligence, telecommunications, cloud computing, and global media corporations. Horizon is chartered as the primary systems integrator responsible for rebuilding, standardizing, and managing global infrastructure.

Horizon assumes operational control over global energy grids, data networks, smart city operating systems, communications, transportation coordination, and large-scale quantum AI governance. Publicly, the company is portrayed as a neutral steward of stability, tasked with preventing the systemic failures that led to World War III.

Internally, Horizon serves as the foundational architecture through which the UFN administers governance, transforming cities into responsive, automated environments optimized for efficiency, security, and continuity. From this point onward, governance and infrastructure become functionally inseparable. Horizon does not exercise formal political authority, yet no system of consequence operates outside its control.

2097: The Chartering of Nova

On December 12, 2097, the United Federal Nations officially chartered Nova. This was achieved after the consolidation of the world's largest biotechnology, pharmaceutical, genetic research, and healthcare organizations. As a result, Nova is granted exclusive authority over global healthcare systems, pharmaceuticals, food safety, agriculture, human genetic research, neural interface development, and longevity sciences.

The charter positions Nova as a safeguard against biological collapse and cognitive decline in the post-war era. Its primary mandate is to extend human life expectancy, mitigate the genetic damage caused by environmental changes, and advance biological and neural integration in line with Horizon-managed infrastructure. These objectives are considered crucial for maintaining long-term population stability and continuity.

While Nova's public mission focuses on prevention and recovery, its classified divisions are engaged in advanced research into human augmentation and cognitive conditioning. Medical systems shift from a treatment-oriented approach to a regulatory one, and biological data become a strategic asset. Consequently, health evolves into a managed condition within the broader framework of global governance.

2135: The Stabilized Global Order

By 2135, after decades of reconstruction, consolidation, and systemic realignment, the world entered a period widely regarded as stable under the combined authority of the United Federal Nations, Horizon, and Nova. Cities across the globe are reorganized into massive megaregions, each encompassing multiple times the geographic footprint of the cities they replace. Vertical construction emerges as the dominant urban model, with structures spanning heights of one to three miles.

These megaregions function as fully integrated smart cities governed through centralized automation with minimal human intervention. Energy distribution, transportation, security enforcement, communication, employment access, and medical care are continuously monitored and optimized. Consequently, for most residents, daily life becomes efficient, predictable, and shielded from the instability that defined earlier eras.

The majority of the global population now resides within these megaregions, having been relocated through a combination of incentives, economic necessity, and enforced policy. Older cities, towns, and rural regions are gradually decommissioned. Outside the megaregions, only a fraction of the population remains, concentrated in automated agricultural zones or dispersed across abandoned territories and nomadic dead zones. Stability is maintained, systems function as intended, and governance recedes from view as authority becomes procedural. Human agency is absorbed into the mechanisms designed to preserve order.

2137: The Baby Boom Reclamation

By the year 2137, the United Federal Nations formally shifted its long-term stabilization strategy toward demographic recovery. A critical threshold for population age is reached after decades of declining global birth rates, exacerbated by war, displacement, environmental collapse, and economic instability. In response, the UFN implements coordinated population growth and family planning initiatives to reverse generational contraction and restore workforce continuity.

To encourage childbirth and long-term settlement, the UFN deploys incentives across megaregions worldwide. Families relocating into newly constructed residential zones integrated into the vertical cities are offered housing guarantees, prioritized healthcare, access to education, and income security. These environments are designed to resemble pre-collapse suburban life while remaining fully embedded within Horizon-managed infrastructure. Children born during this period enter a world characterized by stability and continuous system oversight. Horizon regulates daily life through education pathways, transportation access, and behavioral monitoring. Nova-administered medical systems manage health records, genetic profiling, and cognitive development from birth. Safety and efficiency become normalized conditions. Individual potential is assessed, categorized, and directed long before personal choice emerges, shaping a generation raised entirely within managed systems.

2140: The Great Horizon Fault

On January 28, 2140, the megaregion formerly known as Seattle underwent a catastrophic systemic failure. What became known as the Great Horizon Fault is publicly stated to have started from a localized infrastructure disruption that swiftly escalated across Horizon-managed systems. Within hours, Horizon's city operating system is overwhelmed, bypassing redundancies and triggering widespread power outages. Automated safety measures in place continued to fail, leading to fusion reactor instability, autonomous transportation accidents, and widespread communications blackouts throughout the vertical city. As Horizon's operating framework destabilizes, containment and preservation protocols take precedence over civilian safety measures. Entire sectors are sealed without warning, transit corridors become inoperable, and evacuation systems fail to activate.

Nova-administered medical systems lose synchronization with Horizon's network, severing access to life-sustaining services across multiple population layers. Within days, significant portions of the city become uninhabitable, followed by structural collapse driven by explosions, uncontrolled reactor failures, and cascading infrastructure loss. Official statements continued to push the narrative that the disaster was a confluence of technical malfunctions, environmental stress, and human error. While independent investigations are restricted, Horizon classifies the event as a non-repeatable anomaly, and the UFN designates the Seattle megaregion as a restricted zone. Seattle is removed from all redevelopment and resettlement plans. As a result, public confidence fractures for the first time since global consolidation. While the United Federal Nations affirms that systemic safeguards remain intact, the event exposes the limitations of predictive control and the fragility underlying engineered stability.

2141: The Night of Vanishing Children

On December 22, 2141, less than two years after the Great Horizon Fault, a coordinated disappearance event unfolds across multiple megaregions worldwide. In a single night, hundreds of children vanish from residential zones within Horizon-managed cities. These disappearances occur without any signs of forced entry, system alerts, or infrastructure breaches. Surveillance records are incomplete, corrupted, or later overwritten, leaving investigators with limited information.

Initially, local authorities and the United Federal Nations classify these incidents as isolated anomalies. However, as reports accumulate across North America, Europe, Asia, and the Middle East, investigators begin to identify patterns suggesting coordination rather than mere coincidence. Age ranges, residential zoning, medical histories, and educational tracking data exhibit statistical consistencies that cannot be explained away. The following year, ten children were discovered deceased inside a Nova shipping container at the ports of Dubai. Their remains reveal evidence of prolonged confinement and experimental medical intervention. Despite these findings, official causes of death are not released. Consequently, all investigations are suspended shortly thereafter. Records are either sealed or fragmented across jurisdictions, and references to the event are removed from Horizon-managed civic systems. Public acknowledgment of the incident fades, but for affected families, the event remains unresolved, preserved through informal networks and annual vigils held within the megaregions.

2159: Where The Record Ends

Nearly two decades after a series of devastating events classified as isolated anomalies, the world has settled into what it believes is a state of permanence. The systems endure, the cities stand, and the narratives hold. Public records end here. Satisfied that instability can be identified, isolated, and resolved.

What this story follows is not documented in timelines, inquiries, or sanctioned histories.

It begins within the margins of containment zones, beneath decommissioned city levels, and inside lives whose memories no longer align with the public narrative. It begins with individuals shaped by a world designed to prevent deviation, confronting truths that cannot be optimized away.

The Transition Age is already underway when this story begins. What remains is the cost of believing it worked.

CHAPTER 1

Controlled Testimony

Light barrels into the room, forcing my eyes shut. I squint against the glare reflecting off white metal walls, the brightness sharp enough to sting.

As my vision adjusts, I focus on the man seated across the brushed steel table.

Broad shoulders, rigid posture, and a face set in practiced neutrality. He wears a black suit, a teal tie cutting cleanly through the dark fabric. My arms are locked behind the chair, secured to opposing legs, my posture forced upright for the cameras lining the ceiling. No movement, no sound, just the constant hum of voltage threading through the walls. A sterile white noise that fills the space and leaves nowhere for thought to hide.

The man suddenly kicks his boots onto the table. The impact echoes violently through the room.

He leans back, studying me with casual authority.

"Miss Vale," he says, his voice dry, almost bored.

I don't respond.

"I believe you understand the ramifications that brought you here today." He sinks further into the chair, comforted by the imbalance of power. "But let me refresh your memory."

He pulls a tablet from inside his jacket and unfolds it.

"Let's see," he mutters. "You are being accused of trespassing in a restricted UFN zone…" He pauses, glancing up. "And the murder of a high-ranking Nova executive."

I give him nothing.

He sets the tablet down and leans forward. "Now, let me properly introduce myself." His voice sharpens. "Detective Henry Calloway. United Federal Nations Global Crimes Division."

He crosses his arms, flexing his dominance. I notice the bruises along his knuckles, the skin cracked and raw.

"I'm the only person you'll be seeing for the foreseeable future," he continues. "Possibly the last. Depends on how cooperative you decide to be."

He taps the table once, sharp and deliberate, then gestures toward the sealed soundproof security door.

"I'm the closest thing you have to a friend right now." His voice hardens. "Beyond that door, your fate is no longer in my hands. And it won't be in yours."

He slams his palm down.

"Now!" he shouts. "Do you have anything to say before we begin?"

I lift my head slowly. His eyes are sunken, rimmed with exhaustion. His beard is uneven, streaked with gray. He looks like a man who hasn't slept because remembering is worse than staying awake.

"Miss Vale!" he snaps again.

I stay silent.

The chair scrapes violently as he stands. In two strides, he's in front of me. His hands clamp around my face, cold and damp, forcing my head upward until our eyes lock.

"Do you understand?" he roars. His breath burns against my face.

"Yes," I mutter.

He releases me and steps back, irritation flickering across his face as he regains control. The impression of his hands lingers, a phantom pressure I can't shake.

"Good," Calloway remarks. "Now, are you going to speak? The last thing I want to do is be in this room with you all day."

He rubs his hands across his face, exhaling the stress he's brought on himself.

I look past him at the peeling paint and the spiderweb crack in the tinted observation glass behind his chair. There are only two ways out of this room. One of them ends with Calloway dead.

I turn back to him, holding his gaze.

"My name is Iris Vale."

This is my story.

CHAPTER 2

Containment Breach Protocol

I wake to alarms cycling overhead, red lights slicing through the room in rhythmic bursts.

"Sub-Level breach. Please evacuate to the nearest exit."

The computerized voice repeats between three pulses of the siren.

My mind is fogged, my vision smeared, my body suspended in a numb delay that feels like time itself has stalled. Somewhere beyond the walls, footsteps pound, and voices scream. The sound of people running for their lives bleeds through the corridors.

As awareness returns, the room resolves around me.

A laboratory, with dim perimeter lighting tracing the ceiling. An operating table cluttered with tools sits directly ahead. Vital systems glow along the wall beside me, their displays pulsing steadily, unconcerned.

I'm secured upright in a containment rig. Restraints lock my arms and legs in place. IV lines feed into both arms. Electrodes cling to my chest. A thick cable pierces my shoulder, pulsing with light as it runs into a terminal beside me.

Pain flares sharply.

On the floor near the glass door, a man lies slumped at an unnatural angle, lifeless. Burn marks spider across his body, the smell of ozone heavy in the air. His white lab coat darkens as blood spreads beneath him.

A distant explosion reverberates through the structure. Orange light flashes through the hall beyond the glass. Dust and smoke seep into the room.

The terminal beside me flickers. A red triangle flashes with alerts seared across the screen.

"Life support systems malfunction," An automated voice announces, then the system dies.

A metallic screech erupts behind me as the restraints retract. Sparks shower from the wall. The IVs tear free from my arms, the electrodes adhesive ripping from my skin, the cable ejecting from my shoulder.

I collapse to the floor, pain crashing through me as my body hits hard.

I force myself up and stagger to the man by the door. My hands shake as I search his pockets. I take his phone and a security badge clipped to his belt.

The name catches my eye.

Luc Moreau
Senior Lab Technician

"Thank you, Luc," I murmur.

I press the badge against the security panel. An emblem glows briefly. A solar eclipse, the dark disc perfectly aligned, a radiant corona bleeding outward. Beneath it, a single word glows.

NOVA

The door hisses open. I peer down the corridor. To the right, technicians lie scattered across the floor, unmoving. Further down, a jagged hole has been blown through a dividing wall, fire engulfing twisted rebar and fractured concrete.

To the left, more labs with lights pulsing toward a set of double doors. Above it, a display scrolls.

Loading Bays

I turn left. I brace myself against the glass wall as I move, leaving a streak of blood behind me. My handprints smear along the surface where I try to stay upright.

I stop briefly, catching my breath.

Inside one operating room, a young man lies, limbs hanging motionless off the side of the table. Robotic arms hang above him, scalpels and electrodes poised mid-procedure.

I look away and push on.

Approaching and leaning against the double doors, I slam the badge against a cracked panel. The doors hiss open, and I spill forward into a cavernous storage facility, steel shelving and industrial containers stacked high around me.

I lie still for a moment, staring upward as a yellow strip of light pulses along the ceiling to my right. Rolling onto my side, I spot a bay door torn open at its base, the metal crushed inward as if by force.

I drag myself to my feet and stagger toward it, then crawl through the opening.

The air hits me like a wall, polluted and damp. Alarms continue to echo faintly behind me.

Below the ramp, another man lies crumpled in a reflective jacket, legs crushed. Deep footprints streak the concrete ahead, oil and blood smeared together.

A truck and a car scream past on the underground freeway, the pressure of their passage slamming into me as they vanish down the tunnel. Across the lanes stands a steel door, its surface slashed with red-and-white stripes.

Emergency Exit

The footprints lead straight to it. Another explosion ripples above. Concrete crumbles from the ceiling.

I panic and run across the freeway, bursting through the door. On the other side, I stumble out onto an old sidewalk lining the Chicago River.

The windy night air funnels between the towers, wrapping around me.

I look up towards the glass and steel rising for miles, cascading with light. Maglev trams streak along suspended rails. Lights slicing through the sky.

An AV descends from above, engines roaring, heat washing over me. A spotlight locks onto me as a yellow-striped emergency marker projects onto the ground beneath my feet.

I look up against the blinding light and see armed security guards dropping from ropes before I can react.

In a split second, instinct takes over. I vault the railing and plunge into the dark water below.

The cold shocks my body instantly, as the river swallows me whole.

Voices and sirens blur into muffled noise above. The green-lit water darkens to evergreen as the spotlight vanishes.

My lungs burn. My strength fades as I fight the current.

Time slips away. Then something solid slams into my back.

The hull of a boat floating above.

Hands break the surface and pull me upward. Light fractures through the water.

Then darkness.

I wake coughing, water pouring from my lungs as I lie on the cold metal floor of the small vessel.

A man kneels beside me, steadying my head.

"Hey," he says urgently. "Can you hear me? Are you okay?"

I nod weakly, sitting up as he wraps a dark fleece blanket around my shoulders.

"Catch your breath," he says gently. "You nearly drowned. I thought I hit you."

"I guess I forgot how to swim," I manage to reply.

He gives a small, uncertain smile and glances back toward the city. "I've never seen Nova security this far down before. Those explosions must've shaken something loose."

He looks back at me, at the burns and blood staining my clothes.

"Are you in danger?"

"I think so," I say. "I just... I needed to get out of there."

He nods once. "Okay. Let's get somewhere safe."

He offers his hand. "I'm Cal."

I take it.

"I'm..." My mind blanks. Nothing comes to the surface. "I don't know."

"That's okay," he says, already moving. "We should go."

Sirens howl from above as he starts the boat. A rising hum carries us forward, gliding into the open lake.

I look back as the city rises into view, towers piercing the clouds as far as I can see.

The lights keep shining. The illusion holds.

And somehow, I'm no longer inside it.

CHAPTER 3

Peripheral Knowledge

We drift farther out into the lake, the city pulling away into the dark. I lean against the bench lining the rim of the boat, my arms resting on the edge as I stare back at the lights.

From here, Chicago no longer feels infinite. The towers seem to pierce the stratosphere, their height almost unreal. Bands of light trace the vertical city in ordered layers, each glowing with deliberate purpose. Transit lines and suspended freeways arc between the structures like veins.

Farther out, closer to our vessel, platforms rise several stories above the lake's surface. Broad and evenly spaced, they hold residential districts designed to resemble neighborhoods that no longer exist.

Beyond the city's edge, illuminated agricultural rings curve outward along the remaining shoreline. Controlled and measured, sustaining the life of the city.

I pull the blanket tighter around my shoulders as the night air brushes cold across the water.

Cal moves quietly at the helm. The boat hums steadily beneath us, a constant resonance threading through the lake.

Without a word, he reaches over and offers me a jacket.

I hesitate, then take it.

The fabric is worn but clean, heavy enough to hold warmth.

As I slip my arms through the sleeves, my eyes catch the emblem stitched over the chest.

A clean geometric mark. Interlocking lines cutting through an arc of a sunset. Below it, a single word fades into the fabric.

HORIZON

"Do you work for them?" I ask, my voice still unsteady.

Cal glances back, following my gaze. "Yeah."

He turns his attention back to the vessel's navigation.

"I'm a systems technician," he continues. "Infrastructure side. Mostly maintenance and diagnostics."

"For the city?" I ask.

"For what keeps it connected," he says. "Network maintenance. Aerial and sub-surface links."

He gestures vaguely behind us, toward the river and the disappearing shoreline.

"I was down there tonight scanning the sub-water cables. There's a primary line that runs from here to Milwaukee, another branch that feeds Grand Rapids. Horizon's been watching for any instability, microfractures, signal drift. Anything that might cascade."

"And you just... happened to be there," I say.

Cal meets my eyes briefly. Something guarded passes through his expression.

"Yeah," he says. "I guess I did."

I sit back and look away. His answer feels thin, masking something he isn't ready to share. I let the silence divide us as the boat continues forward, the city shrinking behind us, its lights still flawless from afar.

After some time, the boat slows and drifts into a marina dock jutting out from a cluster of residential complexes lining the far side of the lake.

"We're here," Cal says, cutting the power. He steps off first, then offers his arm to help me stand. As I lean on him, I can feel my body begin to lose strength.

"We can go to a medical clinic inside," he adds as we step onto the dock. "My sister works there, Maeve. She's an attending. She'll be able to help you."

His voice falters slightly as his gaze drops to the cuts and scars along my arms, close enough now for him to see the state that I'm left in.

"It can't be Nova," I say quickly, panic tightening my chest. "The place I escaped from… that's who they were."

"It's not," he assures me as we enter the lobby of the residential complex. The lights inside glow a muted yellow, and the sharp scent of disinfectant hangs in the air. "She helps people who aren't exactly… in the system."

We move toward an elevator corridor. People pass us, some slowing, some staring. A mother pulls her child closer as the girl watches me openly, wide-eyed.

An elevator chimes. The doors slide open to reveal nearly a dozen people standing along the walls. Cal gently guides me inside and taps the panel.

Medical Clinic, Level 62

The doors close. The elevator accelerates in long vertical surges, stopping every few floors as people enter and exit. Finally, a soft chime sounds.

"Level sixty-two," the elevator announces. *"Benton Harbor Medical."*

When we step out, the space feels different, clean, and controlled. Warm white oak panels line the walls, and small trees are placed deliberately across from the clinic entrance, softening the sterility.

Inside the clinic, a striking blonde woman in purple scrubs leans over the front desk, speaking quietly to the receptionist.

"We need to make sure tomorrow's supply delivery arrives on time," she says firmly. "Our community can't go another week without it."

"Maeve," Cal calls under his breath, interrupting.

She looks up, her face brightening at the sound of her brother's voice. Cal nods toward me, and the expression fades instantly when she sees me.

"I need to handle this," she says, handing the receptionist her tablet.

Maeve races from behind the desk toward the clinic's interior doors, opening them for us.

Inside, a circular nurse's station anchors the room, phones ringing softly as nurses monitor screens and speak in low voices. Examination rooms line both sides of the corridor.

At the far end, red doors stand beneath illuminated signs reading.

Aerial Transfer Access

"Exam room five," Maeve says without hesitation, already slipping into command. She turns sharply. "Hey," she calls toward the nurses' station. "I need some help here!"

As I'm rushed into the exam room, my legs finally give out, and I collapse onto the examination table, landing hard against the soft vinyl cushions.

For the first time since the alarms began, I feel the weight start to leave my body. The adrenaline drains away, and with it comes pain. Sharp, radiating, as every nerve wakes at once.

Maeve leans over me, already attaching vital monitors, her movements quick and practiced. Beside her, a nurse struggles searching for a viable vein, fingers steady as she connects a line of fluids to my arm. Cal stands back, helpless, watching without getting in the way.

Maeve grabs a handheld scanner from the wall and runs it slowly along the back of my neck.

The device chirps once, then again.

"Subdermal chip, but I can't get a good reading," she says, glancing up at the terminal screen.

The nurse nods. "Okay, honey. We're going to need a blood sample." She presses a small device around my index finger. A brief sting, then a soft hum.

Maeve turns to the terminal.

The system emits a recursive, uneven sound.

"Oh my," Maeve breathes. "I thought so. The faulty chip was already a bad sign."

Something tightens in my chest. I push myself up on my elbows, instinct screaming.

"Is everything okay?" I ask, my voice thin.

They all look at the screen, then at me.

Maeve swallows. "Iris Vale," she reads carefully. "Missing, presumed dead. December twenty-fifth, twenty-one forty-one."

The room tilts. I can't process the words. My thoughts scatter, colliding with something buried deep beneath them. A flash of memory sears through my mind.

A voice. Soft, familiar, and maternal calling my name.

"Iris," it echoes faintly in my head.

At the edge of the void inside me, the name feels true.

"Iris," Cal repeats quietly, grounding me back in the room.

I look at them, my voice barely audible. "It feels... right."

Maeve pulls a stool close and sits beside me, her expression steady but changed, softer now.

"I'm going to give you something to help with the pain," she says. "Then I'll start treating those wounds."

She taps a panel behind me. "Don't worry," she adds softly. "You're safe here."

Cool relief spreads through the IV, warmth flowing outward as my body finally begins to let go.

The room blurs. And for the first time, I stop fighting it.

CHAPTER 4

What The Body Remembers

For what feels like an eternal sleep, I wake to the sound of whispers. I don't move. I let my eyes peer open just enough to take in the room without signaling that I'm awake.

At the foot of the bed, Maeve and Cal stand close together, voices low.

"Yeah... that's where I found her," Cal says quietly. "I thought I hit her with the boat. I wasn't about to let her drown." He pauses, then adds, trying to justify himself, "She didn't even know her name. Looked like she'd been torn apart by whatever, or whoever she was running from."

"Cal..." Maeve sighs. "You can't keep picking up strays."

He scoffs softly. "Like you don't."

Maeve hesitates. When she speaks again, her voice drops low, sharper now. "There was one other patient. Years ago."

"A teenager showed up at our clinic's door with the same interface sewn into their shoulder," she continues. "His subdermal chip, a ghost. The system listed him as presumed dead." She swallows. "Same date, same markers, same everything."

Cal goes very still.

"The kid looked like he'd seen hell," Maeve says. "Before I could help him, he vanished." Maeve pauses in hesitation.

"The next day, a body matching his description turned up in the agricultural fields north of the West Loop."

"Okay," Cal snaps under his breath. "That's enough."

"I'm just saying," Maeve replies quietly. "Be careful."

I hear her footsteps fade as she leaves the room.

Cal exhales slowly and sinks into the chair beside my bed, rubbing his face.

A moment passes. Then I stir, letting my eyes open fully, pretending to surface from sleep.

"Hey," he says softly when he notices. "I hope I didn't wake you." His voice is gentle.

"It's okay," I reply, slowly sitting myself up in bed.

That's when I notice the room has changed.

The walls are painted in warm, muted tones. A television hangs recessed from the ceiling above me, dimmed to a soft glow.

"Did we move?" I ask, a thread of unease slipping into my voice.

"Yeah," Cal says. "Maeve wanted you somewhere more comfortable. More private." He gestures toward the floor-to-ceiling glass window to my right. I turn my head. "We're a few more levels up, great view from here."

A pale haze hangs over the lake, blurring the city beyond it. Morning light has replaced the chaos of night, revealing a calm that feels almost artificial. The towers stand quieter now, distant and composed.

Below, vehicles hum along the road that divides the building's foundation from the marina. Their sound grows louder as they head toward a tunnel entrance marked.

I-290, Eisenhower Expressway

I look back at Cal.

"How long is she keeping me here?" I ask.

He shrugs slightly. "She's patched you up. Got you clean clothes." He hesitates. "She just wants to try one more thing. Something that might help shake loose your memory."

"Okay," I say, though I'm not sure how much more I can bear to remember.

Cal watches me carefully. "Your name," he says. "When she said it... It seemed like it meant something to you."

"Yeah," I reply. "I can hear a woman's voice sometimes, distant, calling my name." The words feel fragile, like they might break if I press them too hard.

He nods. "Maeve should be back soon," he says gently. "She'll explain what comes next."

I turn back in bed, facing the television as the muted voices sharpen into focus.

"Following last night's breach at Nova's Chicago research laboratory," a female newscaster reports, her tone measured, *"local residents are raising concerns that there may be more to the incident than initially disclosed."*

The screen cuts to live footage along the Chicago Riverwalk. AVs hover between the towers, sweeping bright spotlights across the water as search teams move below.

"This morning, UFN and Nova security forces are conducting coordinated sweeps of the affected areas," the anchor continues. *"Divers report they are searching for missing robotics testing equipment believed to have entered the river during the incident."*

The feed switches to low-frame-rate security footage.

A blast erupts from the lower levels of the Nova tower, a fireball of debris flaring outward into the darkness.

"Witnesses have shared footage from the breach," the reporter says over the recordings. *"Multiple explosions were reported across several levels, extending into the subterranean transit infrastructure."*

The broadcast cuts back to the anchor, her expression more severe now.

"For the time being, transit lines, skywalks, and roadways surrounding the Nova complex remain restricted to authorized personnel only." She pauses, her expression carefully neutral.

"In a statement released earlier today, Nova CEO Dr. Camila Reyes emphasized that there is no confirmed risk to the public and the situation is fully contained."

"Dr. Reyes is urging anyone who may have witnessed unusual activity to report it through official channels, citing an abundance of caution and the possibility that experimental robotic units were damaged or displaced during last night's incident."

The screen dims slightly as the segment ends.

Cal doesn't look at me right away. His eyes stay on the blank display, his jaw tightening.

"That language," he says after a moment. "It's deliberate."

I shift in the bed. "Calling me displaced robotics?"

He nods. "They're building a perimeter around the narrative. Damaged units and displaced hardware..." Cal pauses, his eyes narrowing. "It gives them cover to sweep the city without flagging a person of interest on Horizon's network."

"It wasn't just me," I say, the memory of the loading dock surfacing. "I saw a heavy bay door peeled open from the bottom. Someone else got out first."

I wait for him to say more, but he doesn't. He finally glances at me, something careful in his expression.

"They're looking for something that isn't meant to be public."

The words settle between us, and for a while, a heavy silence crowds the room.

Then a soft knock sounds at the door before it opens.

"Iris," Maeve says softly as she enters the room. "I have one more treatment I think could help you."

She sets a sealed medical case on the table and unlatches it. Inside is an elongated translucent injector, a fine needle extending from its tip. I squint at the sight of it.

"The kind of memory lapse you're experiencing," she explains, "is something I've seen before in patients with severe trauma." She meets my eyes. "This treatment is called Paxim. It was approved after the war to help soldiers, families, and children who survived prolonged exposure to catastrophic events."

She prepares the injector with practiced ease.

"What I'm seeing in you points to deliberate suppression," she continues. "Memories locked away to keep the mind functional. They don't disappear. They wait."

Maeve hesitates, then adds quietly, "I have a patient. He's eighty-seven, a kind man. His family escaped Panama City after the reactor faults. The weeks they spent fleeing the continent, hiding from advancing Russian forces. He witnessed things that fractured him. His mind sealed those memories away to survive."

She looks back at me, steady and certain.

"Paxim doesn't erase pain," she says. "It gives your mind permission to remember it."

For a moment, I sit with the choice in silence. I can keep living inside the pain, hollowed out by what I don't remember. Or I can move forward and risk reclaiming whatever was taken from me. Maybe even find answers to why I was in that lab. Maybe understand how I was able to escape.

I look at Cal. Then at Maeve.

Certain now of my decision.

"Okay," I say. "I'll do it." I swallow as my throat tightens. "What can I expect?"

Maeve steps closer to me, already preparing my arm. Her

movements are careful and precise. "Most patients recall the defining moment," she says gently. "The trauma that forced the memory underground."

She pauses. "The man I told you about... he remembered the moment his sister died. The building they were hiding in collapsed inward. He said the first recall was fragmented. The next clearer. Each time, more vivid than the last."

My chest tightens. I draw in a slow breath and nod.

Maeve positions the injector against my arm. "It happens quickly," she says. "Try not to fight it."

There's a sharp pinch. Then the room dissolves.

The light drains away, and I fall inward into the dark, the void of my own mind.

As the world begins to return to me, I find myself younger, lying beneath warm covers in a familiar bed. My room is decorated with lilies and cherry blossoms. The air smells faintly of vanilla, the quiet warmth of home settling over me like a second blanket.

I feel a hand gently poke my arm, another shaking me awake.

"Iris, my love."

The voice is soft, maternal.

I turn and see her. My mom's face, warm and glowing in the low light.

"Mom?" I ask.

"Yes, my dear," she says, smiling. "Let's go outside. The first snowfall is here."

"Okay, Mommy," I reply, my voice small and sleepy.

I slip my feet into fluffy orange slippers at the edge of the bed. She takes my hand, leading me into the hallway and down the stairs, a blanket wrapped around my shoulders, trailing behind me.

The house is dressed for Christmas. Garlands coil along

the banister, twinkle lights flickering against darkened walls. We pass through the kitchen into the living room, where a Christmas tree glows beside a roaring fireplace. The crackle of burning wood dances with reflections in the ornaments and against the glass of the windows.

"Iris, hurry! We don't want to miss it," my mother says, opening the front door.

A flurry of cold air rushes in.

She leads me down the front steps toward the walkway. Snowflakes drift wildly through the air. At the curb, a black vehicle idles, its windshield wipers brushing away the frost.

Something feels wrong, and I can't shake it. Behind me, I hear my name again.

"Iris?"

The voice is sharper now, clearer. I turn. My mom stands in the doorway. My dad is behind her. Both of them stare at me, color drained from their faces.

"Mom?" I call back.

I look up, trying to understand who is holding my hand.

A snowflake flutters down into the collar of the woman beside me. Her face glitches, colors fracturing into pixels that scatter and fall away. The warmth drains from her expression, replaced by a man's face, tight with fear and determination.

"Iris!" my mom screams from the doorway.

Suddenly, I'm lifted off my feet.

The man throws me over his shoulder and runs. I kick and scream as he reaches the car, shoving me into the back seat before climbing in beside me.

The door slams. The car screeches forward.

Through the rear window, I see my dad chasing us down the street, shouting. My mother's screams dissolve into the falling snow as the distance widens. My dad grows smaller and smaller until the blizzard swallows him whole.

I cry out as the man grabs my shoulder and forces me down.

"Shut it!" he yells. "You're meant for something greater than this."

I fight him, kicking wildly, but he pulls out an injector and drives it into my neck.

A sharp sting and a ringing flood my ears as the memory fractures, light collapsing inward.

The world shatters back into the present.

Maeve and Cal are at the foot of the bed, gripping my legs as my body convulses uncontrollably.

Vital alarms blare around the room.

"Administering Lorazim," the medical system announces.

Within seconds, the violence drains from my body. The shaking slows, then fades.

The pressure in my chest loosens. The world settles back into focus, dulled and distant at the edges.

"It's going to be okay," Maeve says, her voice steady, but tight. "I've only seen reactions to Paxim like this a handful of times."

She leans over me and shines a small flashlight into my eyes. The glare clouds my vision.

She clicks it off, then raises her hand slowly in front of my face.

"How many fingers am I holding up?" she asks.

"Three," I murmur.

"Good." She exhales softly. "Can you tell me what you experienced?"

My head feels heavy, my thoughts slow and slippery. I turn slightly, staring past her toward the window.

"I was asleep," I say. "And then my mom woke me up."

My voice wavers as the images resurface.

"I felt like I was home. Like I was a kid again." I swallow.

"There were Christmas decorations everywhere. A tree, garlands, and lights."

I pause, the unease creeping back in.

"She wanted us to go outside. To watch the snow fall. It was heavy, curling into flurries." My chest tightens. "That's when it stopped feeling like a dream."

Maeve doesn't interrupt.

"There was a car parked out front," I continue. "Running. I didn't recognize it." My voice cracks. "Then I heard my mom calling my name. Iris. Iris."

I shake my head, tears spilling over.

"The woman holding my hand wasn't her anymore. She broke apart. Like she wasn't real." I choke on the words. "Her face faded into a stranger's. The man picked me up and threw me into the back of the car."

I see Cal's jaw tighten.

"The car sped away," I say, crying openly now. "My parents were screaming. Getting smaller. Disappearing into the snow." I press a hand to my chest. "Then the man injected me. It felt as though time stopped."

Silence fills the room. Maeve looks at Cal, then back at me. Her face has gone pale.

"Iris," she says quietly. "You said it was Christmas?"

I nod.

"The date on your record," she whispers. "Your memories..." Her breath catches. "Oh, my god."

Cal straightens. "Maeve. What is it?"

She looks at me like she's seeing me for the first time.

"Iris... you're one of the children."

Maeve's eyes dart to the screen, then back towards me, her professional mask cracking. "The Night of the Vanishing."

Cal's face drains of color. He steps back from the bed, looking between us as if the air in the room has suddenly thinned.

"December twenty-second, twenty-one forty-one," Maeve whispers, the date landing like a diagnosis. "Hundreds of children disappeared from residential zones across megaregions." She swallows hard, her voice trembling.

A cold silence grips the room.

"Most were presumed dead," she adds, her gaze dropping to my arm. "The ones who weren't... they never came back."

A sharp knock at the door shatters the moment. The handle turns before anyone can speak. A shy nurse peeks her head through the opening, her face pale.

"Maeve," she says, her voice barely a whisper. "There are Nova representatives at the front desk." She glances nervously down the hall. "They said a biometric flag was just raised here. They want to verify the record anomaly."

Maeve stiffens instantly, slipping into crisis mode.

"Thanks," she replies evenly. "Tell them I'll be right there."

The door closes.

Maeve turns to Cal and me, concern spreading across her face. "You need to go now," she says in a low, urgent tone. "You must have triggered the silent alert. Nova doesn't just show up."

Cal is already moving. He rushes to my side, gently removing the IV and monitors, before helping me off the bed.

"Here," he says, pressing a bundle into my hands. Folded clothes, a pair of shoes. "Bathroom, go get changed."

Maeve crosses to the terminal and starts typing rapidly, clearing records, scrubbing logs. "The moment I leave this room," she says without looking up, "you run down the hall, emergency stairs only."

She glances back at us. "Go down two floors and exit onto the AV platform."

"I'll have our Medvac pilot, Knox, take you into the city. You'll disappear better there, lost in the noise."

I nod and hurry into the bathroom. Dark green shirt, gray pants, and black sturdy shoes.

My hands shake as I pull everything on, moving faster than I thought possible. I step back into the room, breathless. Maeve looks up, her hand already on the door handle.

"Ready?" she asks.

"Yes," I reply.

Maeve opens the door and holds it wide.

"Go," she says sharply.

CHAPTER 5

Unauthorized Departure

Cal and I sprint through the clinic corridors toward the emergency stairwell, weaving between patients and startled staff.

"There! Stop them!" someone shouts behind us.

I glance back. Two Nova security officers break free from the cluster of reps and clinic personnel Maeve is distracting, their boots already pounding the floor as they close the distance.

Cal slams into the stairwell door and wrenches it open. We take the steps two at a time, the thunder of pursuit echoing down the concrete shaft. A sharp crack snaps past my ear as a taser round ricochets off the wall beside me, bursting into sparks.

Two floors down, Cal points ahead to a set of red doors.

"There!"

Aerial Transfer Access

We burst through them. On the other side, Cal doesn't slow. He pulls a utility knife and slices through the nylon webbing securing a stack of storage crates. With his full weight, he yanks the netting free.

The crates collapse behind us in a violent cascade, slamming into the doorway just as the guards hit it from the other side. Metal shrieks, and shouts follow.

Cal grabs my hand.

Ahead, an AV sits on the pad, engines roaring as heat ripples through the fog. The hatch lifts open, and we dive inside just as the craft lifts, the force knocking us flat against the deck.

The hatch seals.

The engines surge, climbing hard, the force tearing against the sound barrier as we accelerate upward.

"Are you both good?" the pilot shouts from the cockpit.

"Yes, Knox!" Cal yells back, pulling himself upright. He helps me into one of the side seats as the AV angles sharply skyward.

I strap in, my chest still heaving as the g-forces press me back. Across from me, Cal exhales and laughs once, breathless and disbelieving.

Projected flight data etches across the canopy glass.

Destination: Grant Park, Aerial Pads

Beyond the overlay, the lake shrinks beneath us, dark and endless. As we rise, the middle layers of the city come into view. Still pristine from this distance, ordered, untouched.

For a while, we settle into the steady calm of the AV, the constant hum of its engines filling the cabin. Occasional turbulence ripples through the hull, just enough to remind us we're still moving.

A muffled voice crackles over the comms. *"Identify your transport."*

Knox doesn't hesitate.

"An elderly woman and her son," he says easily. "Returning home after a medical appointment."

A pause, filled with static hums.

"All AVs originating from Benton Harbor airspace are subject to inspection," the controller replies. *"Upon landing, remain on the aerial pads for clearance before departing Chicago airspace."*

"Roger that," Knox confirms.

The channel clicks dead.

"Maeve said you two might be in trouble," Knox calls back from the cockpit. "That's probably why air traffic control keeps hailing me."

The hum of the engines softens as the AV begins its descent, slipping into the cloud layer below. For long moments, the city appears only in fragments, steel and light breaking through the white before vanishing again.

Then the engines surge, just as the clouds break apart.

Grant Park's green expanse unfolds beneath us, suspended platforms extending outward from the city's spine, bridging buildings to the open air above the lake. Green spaces and walkways hover in careful symmetry, layered and elevated, alive with motion.

Far below, vehicles race along illuminated paths. People move through their routines, unaware.

"Looks like we've got company," Knox says, nodding toward the landing pad.

I lean forward. At one of the pad exits, several UFN officers stand waiting. The pad itself pulses with expanding yellow rings as we descend, a warning glowing at its center.

Please Wait For Inspection

"When we land," Knox says calmly, "I'll open the rear hatch, and you guys sneak out through the opening. There's a service exit behind us into the park."

The AV settles onto the pad. The engines roar against the surface, smoke billowing as the landing gear locks into place. As the hum cuts out, Cal and I unbuckle in unison, crouching near the rear hatch as it cracks open.

We slip through just as it begins to seal again.

Ahead, Knox opens the front hatch.

"Mandatory inspection," a UFN officer's voice carries over the pad.

"You got it," Knox replies easily.

Cal and I move fast, slipping down a service ramp and into the park below. We duck behind a low retaining wall as a group of UFN officers passes nearby, boots heavy against the walkway. When they move on, we merge into the flow of pedestrians, disappearing into the crowd.

As we walk, Cal nudges my arm and presses something into my hand. A phone, with a Nova keycard stacked on top.

"I found these on you," he says. "When I pulled you out of the water."

I freeze for a moment, then look up at him. "I know I shouldn't have."

"It's okay," he cuts in gently. "I figured it helped you get out."

He hesitates, then continues. "I wiped the phone and moved it onto a dark portion of Horizon's network. Maeve and I are already in your contacts."

He points to a long button along the side. "Press and hold this if you're in real trouble. It sends an SOS. Horizon and UFN will both see it, so only use it if you have to."

"Thank you," I say quietly, slipping the phone away. I hold the Nova keycard a second longer, the name stamped across it burning into my memory. "For getting me out," I whisper, before dropping it into a nearby trash bin.

We continue moving with the current of the crowd until the trees part, revealing the open courtyard of Buckingham Fountain.

"Here," Cal says, gesturing toward a bench along the edge of the perimeter.

We sit and watch the city move. Families drift past. Corporate workers cut through the crowd with purpose. Maintenance crews weave between them, keeping everything in motion. From a distance, it all feels effortless.

Then Cal's phone chirps.

He checks the screen and exhales sharply. "Shit," he mutters. "I just got pulled into another job."

"That's okay," I say quickly, forcing a small smile. "You've already done more than enough for me. I don't expect you to stay."

"Okay," Cal says after a moment. There's hesitation in his voice, like he's weighing what he can and can't say. "But I'll message you later. We'll reconnect."

"I'll be fine," I reassure him. "I'll blend in. Try to find answers."

He nods. "Call Maeve or me if anything goes wrong. We're here to help you."

As we stand, he pulls me into a brief, warm embrace. When he steps back, the feeling lingers. His expression is serious, but kind.

"Good luck," he says. "And stay safe."

Then he turns and disappears into the crowd, leaving me alone beneath the steady spray of the fountain.

I turn and look back toward the lake. In the distance, the neighborhood platforms rise from the water, suspended and quiet against the horizon.

A father and his daughter pass in front of me. She laughs as she skips beside him, her small hand wrapped tightly in his. He slows his pace to match hers, anchoring her movements with an easy, practiced care.

As they move past the fountain, the yellow of her jacket catches the light.

Something fractures inside my mind. For a moment, the present blurs. I see myself there instead, smaller and lighter, running ahead of my dad as we play in front of the fountain. Sunlight scatters across the water, dancing in bright arcs. I can feel his hand in mine, steady and warm, as I skip alongside him, laughter trailing behind us.

The memory doesn't fade this time. It pulls me forward.

I see us walking away together, toward the neighborhood platforms, toward home.

A quiet certainty settles in my chest. "That's where they are," I gasp. My family, my home, that's where I need to go.

CHAPTER 6

The Shape of Home

By the time the sun has climbed to its highest point, I finally reach the neighborhood platforms.

The journey blurs together. Busy intersections humming with traffic, skywalks arcing over tram lines, bridges threading outward from the city's spine. When I step onto the platforms, the scale of them steals my breath, immense, ordered, and surreal.

Homes spread outward in precise grids from central cul-de-sacs, each one a variation on the same design. Different colors, slightly altered layouts, all in distinct Neo-mid-century styles meant to suggest individuality. Though engineered from the same template, every house carries the illusion of suburban life, shaped to resemble the families who live inside.

I walk along the sidewalks as families pass by. Children ride bikes between driveways. Others chase each other across neatly trimmed lawns. Dogs bark somewhere in the distance.

Laughter drifts through open windows. Music and news spill from passing cars as they slow at intersections, traffic lights changing in perfect, obedient unison. The suburb feels alive and familiar.

I pass a house with pale blue siding and white accents, its asymmetrical design broken by large frosted windows.

Something stirs in my chest. A memory presses at the edge of my mind.

I can almost see a boy who lived there, a friend. I remember his laughter, sharp and contagious, the sense that we belonged to each other in that effortless way children do.

The feeling fades, urging me onward.

Ahead, a street sign glows softly along its etched plexiglass edges.

Platform 9F
Fallwater Lane

The name lands like a blow.

My mind fractures. I'm screaming in the backseat of a car, the world blurring past as it speeds away. Snowflakes streak across the windows. At the end of the street, I see it now with painful clarity, my home. Warm amber light glows from wide windows that overlook the water's edge. The Fallwater Lane sign half-buried beneath falling snow.

My chest fills as tears rise before I can stop them.

"My home," I whisper.

Four years of love, warmth, and stability. A childhood interrupted. A life erased the night I vanished from the system.

I quicken my pace.

The early afternoon sun burns away the lingering fog as the house comes into view. It looks smaller than I remember, older. The siding has faded from its once orange color. The lawn bears the quiet marks of neglect. Compared to the vibrant yards around it, the house feels subdued and tired.

But it's unmistakable, it's home.

I slow at the edge of the front walk, my body trembling as I take each step closer. The pain of everything I've lost dulls beneath the clarity of the moment.

A wreath of dying flowers hangs beneath the small rectangular window on the door.

I press the doorbell. A digital chime echoes inside.

Footsteps follow, slow, growing closer. The door opens with a soft creak.

"Dad?" I cry.

He stands there, frozen. Now older and grayer. His frame is still sturdy, still familiar. His face, lined with time and grief, softens as recognition floods his blue eyes.

"Iris..." His voice gives way. "My dear..." His gaze lingers, measuring the distance between who I was and who I've become. Eighteen years stolen, standing between us.

Tears spill freely now, from both of us. I step forward, and he pulls me into his arms with a force that feels like he's afraid I'll leave again.

"It's me, Dad," I say into his shoulder. "I'm here."

He holds me tighter. "I missed you for an eternity," he says.

I don't say it, but I feel the same. So much time has slipped away, leaving a void between us that words can't fill.

After we finally release each other, he steps aside and gestures for me to enter.

Inside, the house feels cold. Not empty, but suspended. As if time stopped the night I vanished and never learned how to move again. The space is slightly unkempt. The quiet neglect of someone who never quite came back to living.

"Here," he says softly, nodding toward the couch.

I sit, sinking into the familiar cushions. The fabric remembers me even if I don't fully remember it.

For a moment, I hear him moving in the kitchen. A kettle whistles. When he returns, he carries two glass mugs, the tea amber with sugar swirling faintly inside.

He hands one to me. The glass is warm and steady.

I take a sip as he lowers himself into the armchair across from me. Behind him, a wide picture window frames the water beyond the yard. The surrounding wall is crowded with photographs. Moments frozen in careful rows. A life documented, then abruptly halted.

"Iris," he says quietly, studying me. "I still can't believe it's you." His voice trembles. "I don't even know where to begin. You were gone for so long. I..." He stops, swallowing hard. "I thought we lost you forever."

He lifts the mug to his lips, the steam fogging his glasses as he tries to steady himself.

"Dad," I say gently. "I know." I hesitate, searching for the right words. "I'm still trying to understand who I am. Where I've been. My memories were locked away." I meet his eyes. "I'm starting to get them back. That's what brought me here."

He nods, blinking fast. "It's okay," he says. "I'm just glad you're here. That's all that matters."

I let my gaze wander, the room slowly becoming familiar. A television mounted above the fireplace, dark and unused. Oil paintings of South Korean landscapes, mountains, and forests, all captured in careful brushstrokes. A glass case mounted along the wall holds a small hanbok, pink and white, embroidered with cherry blossom petals. Small enough for a newborn.

The house holds onto her. But the warmth she once filled it with is gone.

I turn back to him, my chest tight. "Dad... where's Mom?"

He sets his mug down on the side table. The sound feels too loud.

"She never really recovered after you were taken," he says quietly. His voice cracks despite his effort to control it. "She searched for you for years. Filed reports, followed rumors, chasing every lead she could find." His hands tremble slightly in his lap. "But after a while... her heart couldn't take it anymore. And her mind followed."

I feel tears spill over before I can stop them. He doesn't say the words. He doesn't need to.

She's gone. And in some ways, she vanished with me.

After a moment of quiet grief, my dad rises and lifts a small metallic photo frame from the table beside his chair.

He walks over and holds it out to me. I take it carefully, the way you would something fragile, something irreplaceable.

In the photo, my mom and dad stand together in a warm embrace. My dad is dressed in a tailored suit, composed and proud. My mom's wedding gown flows around her, caught mid-motion, light and alive. They are both smiling.

Beneath the image, a short message is written in cursive.

Such love as this is everlasting.
Isaac Vale & Mara Park. July 30, 2134

A slight weight of loss settles over me, but her presence still feels close.

My dad takes the frame from my hands and sets it gently on the coffee table. "Come with me," he says.

He leads the way down the hallway and up the stairs. Along the walls, photographs line the space like an unfinished timeline. Family gatherings, holidays, and friends who drifted away fill the frames. Moments meant to be permanent, preserved in time.

At the top of the stairwell, he opens the first door on the right. The scent hits me immediately, vanilla.

My childhood bedroom has existed separately from the reality I've been living in.

The bright walls of my bedroom are dulled by the sun. My

toys were left where I abandoned them. My bed is neatly made, the covers faintly indented on one side, as if someone spent many nights sleeping there long after I was gone.

I step inside slowly, my fingers trailing along familiar surfaces. I pick up toys, small objects, fragments of a life interrupted. Memories flood back in waves. Hot summer days playing in the yard. Cool autumn afternoons, coloring at the small table tucked against the wall. Winter mornings wrapped in blankets, the world quiet and safe.

My dad leans over the bed and lifts a small stuffed tiger, worn thin from years of being held.

"This was your favorite," he says, placing it in my hands.

I pull it close instinctively, pressing it to my chest.

"Taby," I say, smiling as the name surfaces.

"Sweet Taby," my dad echoes softly.

We move farther down the hall to the last door. My parents' bedroom.

Inside, the bed is unmade. The curtains are drawn, dimming the light. He crosses to the armoires lining the wall and opens them. Inside hang dresses, blouses, jackets, each carefully chosen. Confirmation of a presence that never truly left.

I step closer, brushing my hands through the fabric. Florals, botanicals, all radiating colors she loved.

"I could never bring myself to donate them," my dad says quietly.

He reaches inside and pulls out a beautifully worn brown leather jacket. The lining is a deep purple paisley.

"She's had this since the day we met," he says. "I remember her walking into the restaurant with a group of friends, wearing it over a purple lace-trimmed dress." He pauses, caught in reminiscence. "I thought she was the most beautiful woman I'd ever seen."

On my dad's side of the armoire, suits hang neatly pressed beside college sweatshirts, sports memorabilia, and baseball caps marking every team he's loved and every city he's visited.

I pull a hanger draped with ties from the rack.

"Still working at the same place," he says. "Almost a uniform for private equity in Chicago."

A faint smile crosses his face. A brief moment of relief.

He turns back to my mother's clothes and selects a few pieces to go with the jacket. A cream silk blouse and a pair of purple pants.

"Here," he says, handing them to me. "Take a warm shower. Get comfortable." After a pause, he adds, "Your cousin Lena, if you remember. She still lives in the city and works as a public defender. We can go see her."

"Okay," I say, taking the clothes.

He pulls his phone from his pocket and sends a quick message. "I'll let her know we're coming," my dad says, giving me a faint nod before heading downstairs.

I stand alone for a moment, my fingers sinking into the worn leather and soft silk. The weight of her memory rests in the fabrics. Taking a steadying breath, I slowly cross the hall to my old bathroom.

Inside, pink bath mats cover the floor. A child's toothbrush sits untouched in a yellow glass cup beside the sink.

I tap the wall panel, and the shower comes to life.

As I undress, the borrowed clothes peel away from skin still raw. Adhesive from bandages pulls free slowly. When I look up, I see myself for the first time in the fogging mirror.

My hair is wavy and dark, falling just short of my shoulders. My face looks young, but worn, aged by fear and memory rather than time.

I examine my body. My shoulder is tender where the interface pierces my skin. The cuts Maeve sealed are red and swollen. Scars trace the entire length of my arms and legs, long healed by time. My forearms and thighs are marked with the bruises of restraints. A deep ache settles through my torso.

I step into the shower and slide the glass door closed.

Warm water cascades over me. Soap stings as it finds open skin, the pain sharp but fleeting, replaced by relief. I stay there longer than necessary, letting the heat loosen muscles and quiet my thoughts.

When I step out, the soft pink mats cushion my feet. I dry off with a towel that still smells faintly of fabric softener. I dress, then rummage through the vanity drawers and medicine cabinet.

I brush my hair with a child's brush, rub lotion into cracked skin, and swallow a couple of pain relievers.

Through the bathroom window, I watch AVs streak across the sky above the lake, their lights blinking through the clouds.

I open the door and step into the hallway, steam trailing behind me.

Voices echo up the stairs.

I freeze and press myself against the wall at the stairs' landing, crouching low. In the reflection of a framed photograph across the stairwell, I see them.

Two UFN officers are at the front door. My dad stands between them and the interior, protecting the house.

"Sir, are you certain no one else is here?" one officer asks.

"I'm sure," my dad replies evenly. "My wife passed away years ago. I lost my daughter before that."

The words still hurt to hear.

"All right then," the officer says. "We're canvassing the neighborhood. There have been reports of a woman of interest."

"I understand," my dad says.

"I haven't seen anyone on this end of the street today."

The two officers pause and turn to look at each other.

"Thank you for your cooperation," the officer says. "If you notice anything suspicious, don't hesitate to contact UFN authorities."

The door closes with a soft electronic chirp as the lock engages. Outside, the low hum of a heavy enforcement vehicle fades down the street.

"Iris," my dad calls softly.

I step out from hiding and descend the stairs. He waits at the bottom, worry etched across his face.

"I know," I say. "They've been following me since I escaped."

"It's okay," he says. "We should leave now."

We move quickly through the side door into the garage.

He opens the rear door of the car and pulls a painter's sheet from a nearby shelf.

"Lie down," he says.

I stretch across the back seat as he covers me. The door shuts. The driver's door opens, then closes. The air shifts as the car powers on.

The garage door folds upward as we pull away.

"Iris," my dad says gently, "we're going to be okay. Your cousin Lena will know what to do."

I stay silent, my hands still shaking. In the dark of the back seat, I reach into my pocket and pull out the phone. The screen lights my fingers in pale blue.

Cal, heading deeper into the city.
Found home. Talk soon.

I send the message and let the screen go dark.

CHAPTER 7

Ascent Into Pursuit

After a while of listening to the inner city rush past unseen, the car finally slows to a stop.

"We can get out here," my dad calls back.

I peel the sheet away and sit upright. Beyond the car's windows, the city's underbelly glows in a damp wash of yellow light. Smog hangs thick in the air, clinging to everything.

My dad opens my door. The moment I step out, the smell hits me. Exhaust, oil, and stagnant water, all layered together until my throat tightens.

Around us, underground freeways thunder past, lanes stacked above one another like arteries carved through concrete.

Rows of parked cars stretch into the shadows of the garage, disappearing into darkness.

"We'll take the tram up," my dad says, guiding me toward a wall of sliding glass doors that span the length of the structure.

Above them, a display scrolls.

Cicero District, Sublevel 7
Exit To Tram Station

We move with the crowd spilling from the garage. Voices echo off concrete. Laughter rings sharp and careless. Two men stagger past us, arms hooked under a third as they drag him forward, his feet scraping uselessly across the floor.

Inside the corridor, industrial ventilation roars overhead, blasting cool air downward, forcing the smog back toward the entrance. The hallway stretches endlessly ahead, its walls alive with scattered advertisements.

Pharmaceuticals, food and beverages, luxury brands, and film releases all crowd the walls.

As we descend deeper into the station, the displays flicker in unison. Sound floods the corridor, polished and persuasive.

"When all you need is stability," a voice intones. *"Connection. Freedom."*

Images flash of families laughing, friends gathered beneath glowing towers, people walking confidently through a pristine cityscape.

"Trust Horizon to be there."

The screens fade to white. A stylized sunset glistens at the center, its light perfectly balanced. Below it, a single statement.

Horizon
Connecting You To The World

The words linger as we continue forward, swallowed by the crowd and the hum of the environment.

As we enter the tram station, the ceiling opens into a cavernous arch, seamless panels curving from floor to ceiling in a continuous sweep. At the center of the hall, a towering cylinder rises, wrapped in living screens that display animated maps of the city's transit network. Streams of people rush past, some stopping briefly to study the shifting routes before moving on.

We head toward a bank of escalators leading upward.

At the turnstiles, passengers swipe their phones across angled scanners. I go first, passing my device over the screen. It flashes green.

Fare Paid

My dad follows close behind.

Just beyond us, a cluster of UFN officers stands in quiet conversation, their eyes tracking the crowd. My stomach tightens. I glance at my dad, and he gives a barely perceptible nod. I pull my jacket collar higher, angling my face away as we step onto the escalator. Halfway up, I feel it.

One of the officers is staring straight at me.

"I think that's her," he mutters to the others, his finger lifting in our direction. "The girl Nova's looking for."

My pulse spikes.

I hear a radio crackle. *"Possible suspect identified."*

I grab my dad's hand, squeezing hard. He doesn't look back.

"We need to run," I whisper.

He nods.

The moment our feet hit the platform at the top of the escalator, we sprint.

Ahead, a tram idles, doors open, warning chimes already pulsing. Behind us, officers shove through passengers, boots pounding metal steps.

"Get them!" someone shouts.

Another voice radios, cutting through the chaos. "Suspect on the move."

Passengers cry out as they're pushed aside. My dad and I weave through the crowd, forcing our way into the tram just as the chime peaks and the doors slide shut behind us.

Through the glass, I see the officers reach the platform too late. The tram lurches forward, accelerating smoothly into motion.

We don't stop moving, pushing through two more cars before finally dropping into seats near the rear. The hum of the tram deepens as speed builds, the rails vibrating beneath us.

We breathe, once, twice.

"They'll be waiting at the next stop," my dad says quietly, staring straight ahead.

I nod, my grip still tight around his hand.

The tram accelerates harder, the force pressing passengers back into their seats. Those still standing sway with the shifting angle of the cars, gripping the overhead handrails as the floor subtly tilts beneath us.

Moments later, the speed eases.

"Prepare for Ascent."

The computerized voice repeats as a soft chime sounds. Yellow lights begin pulsing along the edges of the center aisle. Across the windows, diagrams etch themselves into the glass, illustrating the cars separating from one another.

"Please stand clear of tram connection points. Cars will begin to separate in thirty seconds."

The chime repeats in a steady cadence as the tram slows to a near stop.

"Cars separating."

Our car jolts. The front and rear doors seal shut, severing the connection to the rest of the train. Through the glass, I watch one car after another detach, latch onto a vertical steel spine, and shoot upward, accelerating straight through the stacked layers of the city.

Then it's our turn. A deep metallic clang reverberates through the cabin as massive locking mechanisms engage, anchoring us to the vertical structure.

"Ascent to Level 482."

The motors surge. The hum swells into a roar as we rocket upward, floors blurring past in rapid succession.

Each level flashes by with its own distinct character, industrial grit giving way to ordered infrastructure, then to polished steel and muted light. Entire layers of the city vanish beneath us in seconds. Around us, passengers remain unfazed. Some continue their conversations. Others scroll through feeds, read the news, or stare absently ahead, bodies accustomed to the violence of vertical travel.

To them, this is routine. To me, it's unsettling and unreal like being swallowed by the city itself.

I lean against the wall of the tram as it continues to rise, watching the numbers climb along the etched display.

123... 258... 319... 412...

A vertical diagram fills from the bottom upward, a glowing line marking our ascent through the city's measured spine.

The tram begins to slow.

"Disembarking Ascent," the automated voice announces. *"Cars reconnecting."*

Green lights pulse along the center aisle. The display locks onto our destination.

"Now arriving at Elmwood Park Station, Level 482."

I feel the car detach from the vertical spine, a heavy mechanical clunk reverberating through the cabin. Outside the window, articulated arms rotate the tram into position, guiding it back onto horizontal rails. Another jolt as the cars reconnect. The sealed doors slide open between compartments.

The tram lurches forward toward the platform.

At this level, the city breathes differently. The air is clearer. The yellow haze thins, replaced by cooler light filtering through deliberate openings cut into the skyline above. Far overhead, hundreds of levels rise like ribs around a living cavity of sky.

For the first time, the city feels less like a cage. As the tram decelerates into the station, my dad and I stand with the crowd, preparing to disembark.

Through the glass, I see them.

UFN officers, more than ten. Spread across the platform, scanning faces, hands resting near weapons, watching.

The lights in the aisle shift from green to red.

"Please exit slowly," the automated voice intones. *"Security incident reported in the station."*

My dad and I exchange a look. No words needed.

We scan the car, searching for cover, for anything that might let us disappear. Near the front of the car, a group of mothers stands together, strollers clustered tightly. Toddlers nap, one child kicking rhythmically against the footrest, babbling to no one.

One of them wears a brown jacket and navy pants. Close enough.

"Down there," I whisper, taking my dad's hand and guiding him into the center aisle as passengers begin to shift.

The doors hiss open.

We tuck ourselves behind the group as they move forward, their strollers shielding us from direct sight lines. To the right, UFN officers block the main exit turnstiles, funneling passengers through controlled inspection.

To the left, a secondary set of turnstiles remains unguarded, people slipping through unchecked.

"We need to go through those," I murmur.

I wait until the mothers pause near a towering transit map display that juts from the floor.

"Go," I breathe.

We sprint forward, shoving past a startled commuter as the glass panels retract. I pull my dad through the turnstile just as it begins to close, the system chiming in protest.

Behind us, voices rise. I glance back once. UFN officers have stopped the mother wearing the brown jacket.

One of them gestures sharply, confusion rippling through their formation.

We don't slow down. We push through the station doors and spill into the courtyard beyond.

Sunlight floods the space. The glass towers shimmer blue and silver, reflecting a sky that feels impossibly distant. Above us, a massive vertical opening stretches upward, clouds drifting between endless layers of steel and light.

"Where now?" I ask, breath tearing from my lungs.

My dad leans against a concrete wall, taking a moment to steady himself. He grips my shoulder, his hand trembling slightly.

"We're almost there," he says, his voice rough with exhaustion. "Lena's work is just a few blocks over. She'll know what to do."

We move quickly but no longer run, blending into the pedestrian flow. We cross a skybridge into an adjacent pathway, the station fading behind us.

For a moment, the fear loosens its grip. Then my vision glitches, blacking out in random frames.

A sharp ringing overtakes my hearing as a figure bursts from the shadows beside a pharmacy storefront.

Before I can react, a black bag is yanked over my dad's head. I see the flash of a needle, the sharp motion as it's driven into his neck.

"Dad!" I cry.

I lunge forward, but pain explodes at the base of my skull. Something hard connects with the back of my neck, lightning rippling down my spine.

The world tilts sideways. Witnesses scream, their voices collapsing into a distant, distorted roar.

I hit the cement hard, my shoulder absorbing the impact.

And everything goes dark.

CHAPTER 8

Command Override

I wake to distant voices.

"Uncle Isaac, please wake up," a woman pleads. I hear the fabric of her clothing rustling against the floor. "Isaac," she whimpers again.

My dad groans as he surfaces. "Lena... are you okay?" he asks, disoriented.

Before she can answer, her breath catches. "Oh, my God. Iris... is that you?"

Pain sears through my body as my eyes open. I stare upward, blinking against the light. Lena leans over me, her hair falling forward, her arms zip-tied behind her back.

"Iris, honey," my dad says from somewhere behind me. His voice cracks. "Are you okay?"

I try to respond, but my voice is still trapped inside.

I attempt to roll onto my side, but my arms are bound. My wrists burn as the restraints bite into my skin. I shift just enough to see them.

My dad is slumped against a set of overturned desk drawers, his hands bound, his face pale but conscious. Lena kneels in front of me, her legs tied behind her, her eyes tearing with shock.

The room comes into focus.

An abandoned office floor. Rows of empty desks stretch

across the center of the space. Glass-walled conference rooms line the perimeter, running the length of the building. The sun is setting outside, casting long orange bands through the windows. Clouds bruise the sky in purples and maroons as the light drains away.

"Iris," Lena whispers. "We all thought you were dead." Her voice breaks. "I would hug you if I could."

"She just showed up at the house," my dad says softly.

Lena turns back to look at me. She looks so much like my mother, it hurts. Same hazel eyes, same gentle structure. Her hair is now dyed amber, but the resemblance is unmistakable.

"I escaped from a lab," I say, my voice shaking. "They've been hunting me since. I think... they took you because of me."

Lena shifts, struggling to get into a comfortable position against the restraints. "I was just on my way back to the office when I was tased and thrown into a car." She pauses, looking over to my dad, fear edging into her voice. "Next thing I know, I'm here, all tied up."

The silence stretches, heavy with the unknown.

Then, in the distance, an elevator chimes. Hydraulic doors hiss open.

Footsteps follow, echoing into the room, slow and unrushed.

Two figures emerge from the shadows between the rows of desks.

A young woman appears first, blonde, around my age. Her face is scraped and bruised, exhaustion etched into her expression. She wears dark tactical gear, a firearm secured at her hip.

Behind her, a man. Middle-aged with Eastern European features. Short wavy hair, once brown, now streaked with gray. He wears a dark overcoat, trousers sharply pressed, black leather shoes polished to a mirror shine.

"Well," he says pleasantly. His eerily familiar voice turns my stomach. "What a beautiful reunion. The long-lost Vale and Park families."

He stops a few feet away and casually perches against a desk. The young woman leans against a column dividing workstations, arms crossed.

"Who are you?" I demand. "Why are you doing this?"

The young woman scoffs.

"Jules," the man says calmly. "Give her a moment. She'll remember."

He reaches over and switches on a desk lamp.

The sterile white light slices through the fading sunset, illuminating his face.

Gray soulless eyes. Lines carved deep by time and certainty. Weathered hands emerging from beneath his sleeves.

My memory crashes into me.

Snowflakes drifting down. My mother's face pixelating, shattering like glass.

And beneath it... Him.

Rage floods my chest as the present snaps back into place.

His mouth curls into a smile. "Now you remember," he says softly. "Don't you, Iris?"

I stare at him, my hands shaking.

"You stole me!" The words tear out of my throat. "You took me from my family, from my life!"

He sighs, almost offended.

"Stole?" he repeats. "No, I removed you from the mundane!" He sweeps his hand sharply, dismissing my anger entirely. "You, like many others, were destined for far more than the limitations of the generations that preceded."

Lena whimpers as she tries to shift closer to my dad.

The man points toward the woman beside him. "Julien here

is a perfect example of what's possible." His gaze returns to me. "And so were you."

He pulls a tablet from his coat and unfolds it.

The screen lights his face as he steps closer, holding it where I can see.

A 3D scan of my body rotates slowly. *'Nova Labs'* glows in the corner. Lines branch from my brain, spine, eyes, and nervous system.

Enhanced Vision System
Quantum Neural Interface
Reinforced Augmentations
Operative Cognitive Conditioning

IQ metrics, aptitude scores, live vitals pulsing along the side. My heart rate is spiking. Blood pressure is elevated.

I feel hollow, violated.

He begins unbuttoning his overcoat, revealing a black polo and a dark gray lab coat beneath it. The Nova emblem is stitched neatly over his left chest.

"You, Iris," he says calmly, "your mind and physical form were re-engineered for the future."

Silence stretches.

"I know what you're thinking," the man continues, almost indulgent.

"How could this happen to me? What cruelty, what torture!" A faint smile touches his mouth, taunting us. "But your dear friend Elias here only ever wanted to make you the best version of yourself."

He speaks his own name without hesitation, without shame, patting himself on the back.

I strain against the restraints, panic surging.

"There's no need for that, my dear," Elias says mildly.

"You'll be free again," he continues. "Free to return to the path you were always meant to follow." His gaze flicks toward my dad and Lena. "But first, I need you to help cover our tracks."

He draws a knife from a holster beneath his jacket, the blade catching the dying light as he rolls it once in his hand.

"The thing is," Elias says, almost conversationally, "your escape wasn't planned." He steps closer, pointing the knife toward me. "I followed your movements, hoping your conditioning would guide you back."

His eyes narrow slightly.

"But you broke through it." He pauses. "Not sure how. And I would very much like to learn why."

He turns and walks toward my dad, pressing the knife lightly against his throat.

My heart races as I thrash against the restraints, wrists burning. Lena whimpers, her body curling inward.

"So I followed you," Elias continues, unfazed. "I let the leash go a little, just to see where you'd run."

His voice hardens.

"And your father here?" He tightens his grip, the knife pressing closer. "He made it worse."

My nerves go numb as panic constricts my chest.

"That little message to Lena," Elias says calmly, "the one about needing to meet her urgently. It told us exactly where you were headed." The blade shifts, nearly breaking skin. My dad freezes, afraid to breathe. "And it told us what else needed to be removed from the equation."

Elias leans closer, his shadow swallowing us.

"So now," he finishes, "you've brought nothing but mess and baggage with you."

He steps back, releasing the blade from my dad's neck, and returns to stand directly in front of me.

"I never enjoy hurting families," he says, almost regretful.

"But that doesn't mean I won't make the children clean up their own mistakes."

Julien shifts closer to him, silent.

Elias kneels down until his face is inches from mine. I can smell spearmint on his breath.

"So, Iris," he says softly. "Are you ready?" Then, with practiced precision, he speaks the words.

"Fault is not within us."

Something snaps.

A searing pain rips through my skull. A piercing ring floods my ears, drowning out thought. Emotion drains away, pulled clean from my chest.

My body stills, my face empties. I stare at him, waiting. He is in control now.

Julien steps behind me and cuts through the restraints. I rise obediently. No instinct to flee. No instinct to fight.

"You see," Elias says softly, almost fondly, "you were never out of my control."

"Your buttons are just tucked away, locked deep inside."

He pats the top of my head. I don't resist.

"My team trained you to be precise, efficient, and always obedient. An asset designed to serve the higher good." He presses the knife into my hand. My fingers curl around the handle. "A necessary instrument of chaos to maintain stability."

He gestures toward my dad and Lena.

"So," Elias continues, "to correct the course after the mess you've made... I need you to discard the waste."

Something inside me pulls forward. His words guide my body, override my will. I step toward them.

My dad's eyes meet mine. Lena's eyes are wide, shining with terror. They already believe they are dead.

I grab Lena and haul her upright. Something beneath my skin begins to come to life. I lift her clear off the ground, my strength betraying my size.

"Good," Elias murmurs. "Now finish it."

I raise the knife. Holographic images bloom across my vision, markers highlighting Lena's throat as a clear, effective point of entry.

Lena trembles in my grip. "Iris," she cries, her voice breaking. "This isn't you."

Something inside me freezes, straining against the command.

"Don't let him take you again," Lena pleads, her eyes locking onto mine. "Your mom never stopped looking for you. Not for a single day."

I can't hold her gaze. My hands begin to waver.

"Aunt Mara kept your room exactly the way you left it," Lena chokes out. "She slept in your bed waiting for you to come home." The words hit like a fault line.

The consuming darkness of Elias's control fractures. Through the cracks, my memory bleeds in cold and sharp.

Snow is falling on a black car. A hand slipping from mine. My mom screams my name as she disappears into the white.

"Iris." The voice isn't Lena's. It's softer, closer, and maternal. "Iris, my love."

My vision begins to flicker. My arms hesitate, losing strength.

Julien moves in behind me, and my control snaps back.

Time slows as my vision locks onto Julien. I release Lena, dropping her to the floor. My movements scale faster than Julien can react. I drive the knife hard, twisting it into her side. Julien screams as I collapse with her.

Elias lunges forward.

I rip the gun from Julien's holster as I roll. Holographic markers lock onto Elias's leg as he charges.

I fire. The suppressed shot cracks through the office in a sharp, contained burst.

Elias shouts, clutching his leg as he crashes to the floor. Julien writhes nearby, choking on pain.

I tear the knife free from Julien and rush back to my dad and Lena, cutting their restraints. Together, we pull him upright and stagger toward the elevator bay.

Behind us, Elias drags himself forward.

"Iris!" he shouts, fury bleeding through his voice. "This isn't over."

The elevator doors slide open. We spill inside.

The doors seal as the lift descends rapidly, escaping their vengeful reach.

CHAPTER 9

Breaking Altitude

Inside the elevator, the three of us struggle, heaving as we try to catch our breath.

"I'm so sorry," I say, my voice breaking. "I had no idea."

Lena wipes at her face, trying to steady herself. My dad leans against the wall, pale but upright, forcing himself to stay present.

"I know," he says quietly. "I just..." He exhales. "I can't fathom what you've been through."

The elevator slows.

Applied Capital Lobby, Level 900

The chime echoes softly as the doors hiss open.

We step into a dim, nearly deserted lobby. Beyond the glass walls, the sidewalks are alive with motion. We don't hesitate. We merge into the crowd, putting distance between us and the building.

The night sky stretches open, no layers or thresholds above us. Just towers ending against the dark. The moon reflects off the glass and steel. At this height, the city feels different, cleaner, and untouched.

Pedestrians pass in tailored clothes, children tucked close at their sides. Workers drift toward restaurants and apartments.

Laughter and faint music spill from cafés and bars lining the walkways. As we walk, I pull out the phone.

3 Missed Calls
2 Messages
From Cal Rowan:
Call me when you can.
Just need to know you're okay.

I press call.

Cal's face appears on-screen almost instantly. "Iris," he says, relief flooding his voice. "Are you okay?"

"I think so," I reply, unsure how true that is.

We pass a glowing waypoint marker rising from the pathway.

Fulton River District

"Good," Cal says. "Maeve told me what happened at the clinic. Nova put her through hell, but she's okay."

He shifts the camera. The view swings wildly before settling. Cal is suspended by a harness, clinging to the side of a tower. Behind him, rows of rectangular antennas hum softly, the city sprawling beneath.

"Pretty wild, right?" he says, forcing a grin.

"Cal," I interrupt. My voice tightens. "We need help."

His expression changes immediately.

"I found my dad," I continue. "And my cousin. We've been running from UFN officers, and..." I hesitate. "A man from Nova. He's the one who abducted me."

Cal goes still.

"I think they're using my chip to track me," I say, touching the base of my neck. "It's monitoring my biomarkers. It knows exactly where I am."

"I've got you," he says firmly. "I'm sending a signal now. It'll scramble local emissions around your phone. It won't last forever, but it should buy you time."

"Okay," I breathe, the invisible weight lifting slightly. "We'll stay somewhere public and lay low. But we need to leave the city tonight."

"Do that," Cal replies. "Once you're stable, message me. I'll get to you."

The call ends.

Lena steps closer. "New York," she says quietly. "I have a friend there, high-level at Horizon's media division."

I look at her in hesitation.

"It's safer," she adds. "If we stay among people who are already protected."

I nod, tightening my grip on my dad's hand as we disappear deeper into the crowd.

After what feels like an endless walk, our pace finally slows. We're tired and worn thin. Ahead, the upper levels begin to taper toward the city's edge, where the towers thin and Lake Michigan looms, a vast black void beyond the glass and steel horizon.

Lena guides us farther along and into a nearby 24-hour café, its windows glowing warmly with candlelit tables.

We settle at a table a few seats from the door. The restaurant wraps around us in deep maroon tones, walnut table tops polished smooth by years of use.

My dad slouches as he slides into the wall-side booth, exhaustion finally winning. I sit close, letting him lean against my shoulder.

For a while, none of us speaks. The weight of the last few hours hangs heavy between us.

A young waitress approaches, stopping at the edge of the table. "What can I get you all tonight?"

Lena leans back slightly. "Can we start with some coffee for the table?"

"Of course," the waitress replies with a long stare before walking away.

Lena looks back at me. My eyes are barely staying open. Beside me, my dad has already drifted off, snoring softly against the booth.

"I guess we all look like hell," she jokes quietly. Then her expression hardens. "I don't like being stationary. We're sitting ducks here." She glances toward the glass facing the street. "We need to get to the airport soon."

I nod. "Staying here isn't safe." I hesitate, looking at the suspended rails outside. "But we can't take the trams. After what happened at the station... If we step back onto the grid, they'll find us."

The waitress returns, placing a tray of mugs in front of us. Steam curls upward as she sets down a small pitcher of creamer and a handful of sugar packets before smiling and moving on.

I wrap my hands around my mug, the warmth seeping into my palms, and take a slow sip.

"So," Lena asks, tearing open sugar packets and dumping them into her cup.

"Who was that you were talking to on the phone earlier?"

"Cal," I reply. "I met him after I escaped. He pulled me out of the river."

Her eyebrows lift. "Seriously?"

"He brought me to a clinic to recover," I continue. "That's where I met his sister, Maeve. She's an attending there."

Lena smirks. "So you already met the family."

"It wasn't exactly a social visit," I mutter. But her words pull my mind back to the promise he made at the fountain. I pull the phone from my pocket and wake the screen, typing quickly.

Hanging low at a café.
Need to get to New York.

Seconds later, the reply appears.

Okay. I'll be there shortly.
Pinging your location now.

I set the phone face down on the table. Lena tilts her head. "Calling reinforcements?"

"I just know Cal can help," I say.

We sit there a while longer, letting the coffee work through our exhaustion. Lena starts talking, filling the quiet with childhood stories and life events I missed.

"You wouldn't believe how many Parks moved back to Seoul once all the nieces and nephews finished university," she says, a warm laugh escaping her. "My parents were just ready to live in peace. They ended up settling down not too far from our grandparents, right on the outskirts near Anseong."

For a moment, listening to her talk, it almost feels normal.

But then her smile falters. "I spent a lot of time with your mom and dad toward the end." My chest tightens. "She was such a light, Iris. But I always felt like she was hiding how much losing you broke her."

Her eyes glisten. "Your dad took such good care of her. I used to tell her all the time how lucky she was." She exhales, her voice trembling. "But, after she passed... the silence was too loud. We all ended up abandoning him in grief."

"I always loved when you visited," my dad says gently, reaching across the table to ease Lena's guilt. His voice is rough but steady. "You didn't abandon me."

"I can't help but feel responsible," I say quietly.

I look between them, realizing how misplaced all of our guilt really is. The blame doesn't belong to anyone at this table. My mom's death and my dad's loneliness weren't failures of love. They were collateral damage from the night Elias shattered our lives.

Then the door opens, and I look up just as Cal steps inside. He's dressed casually, a backpack slung over one shoulder. He spots us and waves before walking over and sliding into the seat beside Lena.

"Hi," she says, offering her hand.

"Hey," Cal replies, shaking it. "You must be?"

"Lena Park," she cuts in with a grin. "Iris's favorite cousin."

Cal smiles, easing into the dynamic instantly. He leans across the table to shake my dad's hand. "Nice to meet you, Mr. Vale."

He settles back, his expression shifting from polite to focused.

"So," Cal says, "I hear you need to get to the airport."

We all look at him.

"I've got us a ride," he adds confidently. "Whenever you're ready."

Relief floods through me. "Thank you, Cal. The sooner, the better."

He pulls out his phone and taps the screen. "Knox, we're heading your way."

A muffled voice answers. *"Copy that. Ready for departure."*

As we stand, I help my dad up. Lena quickly swipes her phone across the embedded payment screen at the edge of the table.

Outside, the night hums. Traffic flows toward a descending ramp as we follow Cal down the sidewalk. He points ahead.

Montrose Aerial Pads Access, Level 902

We pass through the security gate and climb a short set of stairs. On the pad, the familiar Medvac AV awaits, engines roaring. The hatch hisses open.

Knox helps us inside, guiding us to seats along the walls.

We buckle in just as the hatch seals shut. The engines surge, lifting us skyward.

Across the canopy glass, a glowing waypoint appears.

Destination: O'Hare Airport

The AV ascends, lifting cleanly above the city. At this height, we glide over the tops of the buildings themselves. I press closer to the glass, staring down at Chicago spread beneath us.

The roofs are crowded with infrastructure. Satellite arrays and dense clusters of antennas link the city. Massive HVAC systems pull air up through the towers. Between them, dark openings plunge downward where the river arteries cut through the concrete, channels disappearing into layers far below.

On the opposite side of the cabin, I hear Cal talking with my dad.

"Thank you," my dad says quietly. "For all of this."

"No problem," Cal replies. "I'm just glad I could help."

Lena nudges my shoulder and gestures ahead.

In the distance, beams of light spear upward into the sky from the city's Horizon tower, rising higher than the rest, piercing the cloud layer. For a while, we float among the clouds, navigation lights blinking as other AVs and jets slide past us, ghostlike and silent.

I see Cal unbuckle himself from his seat and walk toward me, his bag slung over his shoulder.

"Hey," he says, sitting down beside me. "I picked up a few things to help you."

He reaches into his bag and pulls out a small scanner device, turning slightly toward me. "This should disable your subdermal biomarker."

I nod and shift in my seat, turning my back to him. I tilt my head down as his hands gently brush my hair aside.

He waves the device along the back of my neck. A few soft chirps sound, followed by a sharp sting that shoots through my spine.

The device echoes, *"Biomarker disabled."*

I turn back toward him, rubbing the back of my head. He places the scanner back into his bag, then holds out his hand again. This time, a small pill bottle rests in his palm.

"Maeve wanted me to give this to you," Cal says, handing it over.

I take it carefully and read the label.

Paxim Nightly
Take one capsule as needed before bed
Do not exceed one dose in 24 hours
Prescribed To: Iris Vale

"What's this for?" I ask, uneasy at the thought of taking it again.

"Maeve thinks it might help you remember," he says, trying to reassure me. "It's not meant to overwhelm you. She said it just helps surface memories through your dreams. The ones your mind is already trying to reach."

He leans closer and gently folds my fingers around the bottle. "She just wanted me to warn you. Sometimes the dreams can alter the memory. Hide parts of the truth."

I pull back slightly and slip the bottle into my coat pocket. "Okay," I say with a small nod. "I trust her. I just don't know if I trust what I'll see."

We settle back into our seats, the space between us filled with quiet tension.

Before long, the engines begin to ease back. Below us, the airport comes into view.

The terminals form clean geometric patterns, runways weaving between structures and extending out over the edge of the city's highest layer. It's surreal watching hypersonic jets launch straight off the city itself, their runways suspended more than two miles above what used to be ground. Each aircraft briefly drops into the clouds before roaring upward into the stratosphere, its engines burning with blue fire.

The AV settles onto an aerial pad just outside one of the terminal buildings. Landing lights project beneath us as the gear locks into place.

The hatch opens, and we unbuckle, stepping out into the controlled chaos of the terminal entrance. Inside, travelers surge past in every direction. Bags weighing down their shoulders.

Suitcases rattling across the floor. Voices echoing against glass, marble, and steel.

We stop just short of the security checkpoints.

Cal pauses and pulls out his phone, motioning us into a loose circle. "Alright," he says, tapping quickly. "I'm sending your boarding passes now."

A soft chirp sounds, and all our pockets buzz at once.

I pull out my phone. The boarding pass glows on the screen, crisp and official.

"You should be clear through security," Cal says, trying to sound confident. "I checked your records in the Horizon system logs. No UFN warrants, nothing flagged."

He looks at each of us in turn. "By inter-region travel law, UFN can't detain anyone inside an airport unless there's a direct threat."

"So, just blend in?" I reply.

"Yes..." He pauses with a small smirk, "Just don't get into any trouble."

I nod in defiant agreement.

We follow behind him toward the security checkpoints. UFN officers stand posted at either end of the passenger lanes, their presence rigid and watchful. Travelers funnel forward, placing bags onto conveyors that vanish into the walls. One by one, passengers step through tall archways glowing green as biometric and CT scans are completed.

I can feel eyes on us as we move.

When it's my turn, my pulse spikes. I step through the archway.

A sharp chirp sounds. The light shifts from green to yellow.

My stomach drops.

The UFN officer at the terminal glances up, frowning at her screen. Then she waves me forward. "Continue moving," she says flatly. "Ex-military always flags the scan. Hardware variance. More than standard augmented prosthetics."

I nod quickly, not trusting my voice, and move on before she can reconsider.

Beyond the checkpoint, Cal waits as his bag reappears from the wall. My dad and Lena stand nearby, already clear.

"That was... strange," I murmur to Cal.

"Hm?" he says, checking his pack.

"The officer said I was ex-military."

He looks up, puzzled. "I don't see any visible augments," he says quietly, studying my arms.

Then something shifts in me as a cold realization sets in. I think of Elias's experiments, the reinforced augmentations, and the neural interface.

I look down, envisioning the machinery hidden beneath the scars running the length of my arms and legs.

"I think it's under the surface," I reply. The thought makes my skin crawl.

I begin to question if what lives inside this body is even me anymore.

Cal's expression tightens. "If that's true..." He exhales.

"I've never seen anyone with augments like that." There's a trace of awe in his voice. Then his tone lightens as he shifts focus. "Right now, let's just not miss our ticket out of here."

We move down the terminal's long corridors. Cafes and concessions glow along the edges.

Travelers hurry past, others wait in clustered rows of seats. Outside the glass, aircraft line the taxiways, humming softly beneath the lights.

Each jet gleams with bold livery, the word *'STRATOS'* emblazoned across its fuselage.

At the gate, a calm automated voice announces, *"Now boarding. Flight 4963 to New York, JFK Airport."*

We join the line, swiping our phones against the panels. Soft chimes echo as we descend the jet bridge.

Inside, the cabin is full. Rows of three-seat sections stretch ahead, overhead bins snapping shut as flight attendants assist passengers. The aircraft hums steadily beneath our feet.

I take the window seat. My dad and Lena sit beside me. Across the aisle, Cal settles into his seat.

The screens embedded in the seatbacks flicker to life, looping the Stratos welcome animation.

Soon, the plane door hisses shut, and we begin taxiing. The seatbelt chime sounds as the terminal recedes behind us.

The pilot's voice comes over the intercom. *"Thank you for choosing Stratos for your flight to New York City. Weather conditions are clear, and we expect a smooth journey. The estimated flight time is thirty-five minutes. Sit back and enjoy."*

The engines roar as we roll onto the runway. Then we're airborne.

The city drops away, lights slipping toward the edge of the world. For a breathless moment, the aircraft dips, then the engines surge, hurling us forward as we climb, brushing the stratosphere.

When the g-forces ease, I rest my head against the curve of the window.

Chicago fades into darkness below. The horizon curves ever so slightly, the sky deepening into navy as the moon hangs above.

For the first time in hours, something loosens in my chest. We're still running. But for now, we're moving forward.

CHAPTER 10

Heights of Order

On time, we land in New York, the aircraft descending from the sky toward a massive platform suspended above the Atlantic, southeast of the city's core.

The jets throttle down, reverse propulsion flaring as the landing gear meets the runway.

Ahead, the airport unfolds in a radial grid of gleaming terminals. At its center, a colossal superstructure rises and twists skyward, a sculpted spine of glass and steel. Suspended freeways and transit lines radiate outward from it, threading into the surrounding layers of the city.

Even from here, the density of New York eclipses Chicago.

"We'll be arriving at the gate soon," the pilot announces over the intercom. *"Local time this morning is seven-twenty-three, October twelfth. Today's forecast calls for slight overcast, with temperatures holding at fifty-two degrees. UFN has issued a high wind advisory for the upper levels. Please take precautions."*

The aircraft taxis to the gate. Green guidance lights pulse along the center aisle as we disembark, passengers funneling forward in a slow, collective drift. Overhead in the concourse, paneled spines of maple wood arc above us, lights embedded along helices of glass that spiral through the ceiling.

Lena steps ahead, suddenly energized.

"Okay," she says with a grin. "Now we're in my territory."

She moves with confidence. "I spent my university and law school years here. I always love coming back."

We follow as she leads us across massive skywalks connecting the outer and inner terminal rings. Crowds stream around us, efficient and endless. Above, through the glass canopy, the central superstructure looms higher and higher, its silhouette like a torch piercing the sky.

At the airport's core, we clear turnstiles and security checkpoints before entering the tram station.

The scale is overwhelming.

Forty tram lines intersect across multiple platforms. The trains themselves stretch twelve cars long, sleek and humming with energy.

"Here," Lena says, guiding us toward a train pulling in.

A curved display above the platform scrolls.

Green Line: Manhattan Center, East 79th

We board and take seats along the outward-facing row. My dad and Lena sit together. Cal and I settle in behind them.

The tram accelerates smoothly, curving downward into a tunnel beneath the superstructure. Around us, multiple lines converge along a massive vertical steel spine that disappears upward for hundreds of feet.

At staggered intervals, tram cars detach, latch onto automated arms, and peel away. Each one snaps into position before rocketing skyward.

A familiar chime echoes through our car.

"Please stand clear of tram connection points. Cars will begin to separate."

Our section unlatches from the group. One by one, the remaining cars vanish upward into the city above.

A heavy metallic clank reverberates through the cabin as the locks engage, shifting our car into position. Electric motors surge, roaring to life, and we're launched straight up into the structure.

The acceleration pins me to my seat.

Moments later, the vertical lift slows. The cars reconnect with a suspended rail, the force easing as we transition from ascent to forward motion.

Our tram emerges from the airport's superstructure onto an elevated transit line angled sharply upward into the upper layers of the city.

I watch in silence, my reflection ghosted across the glass.

Far below, the ocean disappears beneath the muted glow of early morning light.

Ahead, the city's illumination grows stronger, denser, swallowing the horizon. As we approach Manhattan's outer edge, the city curves upward around us, rising vertically in impossible tiers.

The protected airspace comes into view. The Statue of Liberty and the World Trade Center are still intact, but now dwarfed by the city that towers around them. The skyline curves inward, its staggering height bending away by design, stopping just short.

Moments later, the tram is swallowed by a dense structural threshold separating the city's upper layers from everything below. The rising sun slips out of view behind us as the cabin fills with artificial light.

"Now arriving," the automated voice announces over the intercom. *"East 79th Station, Level 897."*

The tram decelerates smoothly, drawing us into the station. We rise into a vast glass dome, its curved ceiling lined with suspended lights and cascading display panels that glow softly overhead. We disembark and move into the terminal beyond.

A spine of white marble arches upward through the space, pulling the eye toward the exits and the city waiting beyond them. The environment feels different here, vibrant, a false freedom from decay.

Outside, the station opens into elevated parkland. Grass-lined paths and clusters of trees sway gently in the wind, their canopies igniting in shades of amber. Greenery spills outward along the perimeter as if reclaiming the structure itself.

Around us, towers climb into the sky. Sunlight glints off blue, white, and green-tinted glass, chrome-plated steel, and pristine concrete. Everything feels intentional, curated.

"Let's stop here," Lena says, sitting on a marble bench that runs along a retaining wall holding a raised garden of flowers. "I'll call us a car."

We sit in silence as we wait.

My dad settles beside me and lets out a slow breath. "I remember coming here when I was a kid," he says quietly. "They were in the midst of constructing this layer of the city."

He lifts his arm and gestures toward the parkland stretching beyond the multilane roadway. Wide lawns, winding paths, artificial lakes, and trees arranged with careful intention.

"Contested," he says. "A mirror image of the old Central Park."

He pauses, watching people pass beneath the shade. "I guess even the ultra-wealthy still need something that feels grounded."

Cal's phone then rings. He answers immediately.

"Hello?"

Maeve's voice filters through the speakers, soft but urgent. *"Did you make it there okay?"* she asks, the concern in her tone unmistakable, like an older sister who never stops worrying.

"Yeah," Cal says, glancing around. "We just got into the city." A faint smile tugs at his mouth.

"It's... incredible. We'll have to come back here someday."

"Maybe this spring," Maeve replies lightly. *"Though I don't think Mom wants us skipping the annual family reunion in Sydney."*

The color drains from Cal's face. She's struck something deeper than she knows.

"Okay, Maeve," he says quietly. "I'll keep you posted."

The call ends.

Ahead of us, a large black SUV hums to a stop at the curb. Lena stands and waves an arm.

"Car's here!" she calls.

My dad and I exchange a glance, neither of us quite sure what we're stepping into next.

The driver exits and opens the rear doors. Lena slips into the front passenger seat. The three of us settle tightly into the back of the luxury vehicle.

Inside, screens come to life, displaying a live map of the city. A waypoint pulses in the distance. Blue chevrons project onto the windshield, guiding the road ahead. Soft music hums through hidden speakers, low and unobtrusive.

The door seals shut with a solid, reassuring thud.

"Good morning," the driver says as he takes his seat. "Glad to be of service. I'll be taking you to Sentinel West Tower." He glances back, confirming.

"Yes, sir," Lena replies.

The SUV pulls forward, gliding along a road that cuts cleanly through the park. Halfway across, the ground drops away. The road becomes a bridge.

I look out the window.

Below us, the city layers unfold, dense and alive. The light shifts darker, tinged yellow and industrial, a stark contrast to the pristine levels above. New York, stacked upon itself, divided by progress.

As the park reforms around us, the ground solidifies beneath the vehicle, and the road straightens into a clean grid on the opposite side. The car slows as we pull into a valet port beneath a tower that rises like an immense spire of emerald green glass.

Above us, starbursts of gold-brass and bright white light glisten, accenting fluted marble walls that frame the building's entrance.

We step out and move inside.

The lobby opens wide and luminous. A café lines the right side, already alive with morning workers preparing for the day. The space is filled with avant-garde furniture in warm earth tones, punctuated by sharp dark-green accents. At the center, a regal reception desk anchors the room.

Lena strides forward without hesitation.

"Hey!" she calls out. The receptionist looks up, recognition lighting her face.

"It's been a while!" The receptionist replies with a grin. "Back to stay with Benjamin again?"

"Totally," Lena says easily. Then she gestures over her shoulder. "And I brought some friends and family."

The receptionist's eyes flick toward us. For a brief moment, her smile tightens. We look painfully out of place, travel-worn, clothes rumpled, carrying the residue of places we shouldn't have survived.

"Got it," she says after a beat.

She types rapidly at her computer, then reaches beneath the desk and produces a velvet-tied envelope, sliding it across the surface.

"Your temporary keys."

"Thanks, girl," Lena says, scooping it up. "We'll catch up soon."

The receptionist nods as Lena rejoins us.

From the envelope, Lena pulls out a set of translucent keycards and hands one to each of us.

"You'll need these to get anywhere in the building," she says, holding her own up between two fingers. "Top-tier access."

She smiles, but there's an edge to it.

"Okay," I say, holding the card up to the light. Inside the translucent material, a barely visible map of New York City is etched into the fine layers.

"Follow me," Lena replies, already moving.

She leads us toward a bank of elevators set into a curved stone wall. She taps the control panel, and a soft pulse of light confirms the call. Moments later, a chime sounds and the doors glide open.

Inside, white oak panels line the walls. One side is frosted glass, wide and seamless, with a display screen embedded beneath the surface. Soft lighting traces the ceiling, warm and steady. Lena steps in front of us and taps the panel, selecting Ben's floor.

Level 941

The elevator hum deepens as it accelerates upward, the pressure settling gently into my chest. Dozens of floors pass in seconds before the motion eases.

The doors slide open.

We step into a pristine hallway, quiet and softly lit, the air cool and still.

Lena leads us to the end of the corridor and stops at a door marked.

Unit K941

She presses the doorbell and knocks.

From inside, a voice calls out, "I'll be right there!"

The lock disengages, and the door opens slowly, revealing Ben. His hair is neatly styled, still holding the sheen of someone who just finished getting ready for the day. He wears a tailored cotton suit in light beige, layered beneath a deep brown button-down. His trousers end just above the ankle, revealing intricately patterned socks.

"Reception said you were here," Ben says, pulling Lena into a hug.

His gaze shifts past her shoulder, landing on us.

Cal lifts a hand. "Hi."

"And it looks like you brought company," Ben adds, mild annoyance creeping into his voice.

"Long story," Lena says quickly. "I'll fill you in later. We just need a safe place to lay low for a bit."

Ben studies her for a moment, then exhales, his soft spot for her winning out.

"Well," he says, stepping aside, "you're always welcome."

He gestures us in.

The door closes behind us as we move down a short entry hall that opens into a vast main living space. Floor-to-ceiling windows stretch across the far wall. To the left, a sunken living area sits bathed in natural light. To the right, an immaculate kitchen gleams, every surface pristine, designed for someone who actually uses it.

"Benji," Lena says softly as we approach the windows, "Your place is beautiful as always."

Outside, the upper reaches of New York extend beyond the horizon. Layers of manicured green space weave between towers of glass and steel.

Beyond them, the new Central Park cuts a wide, open corridor through the heart of the city.

I turn back to see my dad already settling into an armchair, the tension easing from his shoulders as he finally allows himself a moment to rest.

"So," Ben asks, setting a tray of glass mugs on the counter. "What brings you all the way out here?"

We each take one. The coffee smells rich, intentionally crafted.

"We needed to get out of Chicago," I say carefully, still unsure how much to reveal.

We drift toward the kitchen island. Lena drops onto a barstool opposite us and lifts her wrists theatrically.

"Some man and a crazy bitch held us captive," she says. "Like this." She mimics restraints.

Ben stares at her. "You're kidding? Right."

"No," Lena replies, her eyes glaring down his doubt.

"Look at her arms, Ben."

Ben's gaze drops to my arms peering out beneath my jacket sleeves. He sees the lines of my scars, the fresh bruising around my wrists where the zip-ties had cut into the skin. His expression shifts from skepticism to something colder.

"I escaped from a lab beneath the city," I say, my voice steady but hollow. "It was Nova. There were others, bodies left cold in the corridors."

The image flashes in my mind. The lab techs sprawled across the floor, the firelight glistening eerily off the glass walls.

"I made it out," I say, nodding toward Cal. "That's where he found me."

Cal lifts his mug slightly in acknowledgment, his face grim.

"My memories were locked away," I continue. "But they're starting to resurface now." I look up at Ben. "The man who took us... he called himself Elias."

Ben goes very still, his casual charm vanishing entirely.

"Elias," he repeats, the name landing heavy in the room.

He sets his mug down, the chime of the glass distinct against the stone counter. "Elias Mercer?"

My stomach tightens. "You know him?"

"Everyone in the media feeds knows of Elias, but no one ever speaks to him," Ben says, his voice dropping low. "He's a Senior executive at Nova. Old money, old blood." He looks at me, his mind racing. "His family founded one of the German biotech firms that got absorbed when Nova was chartered."

He pulls out his phone, types quickly, and turns the screen toward me. The image glows dark against the sunlight spilling through the windows.

Elias stands amongst a group of monolithic executives, perfectly pressed suit, polished shoes, dark, lifeless eyes.

"That's him," I confirm.

"We've been getting rumors in the back-channels for years..." Ben pauses, gauging if what he says next breaks confidentiality. "People suspect that he had his own wife and son killed during the chaos of the Horizon Fault in Seattle."

Ben exhales sharply, running a hand through his hair. "If Mercer is surfacing, if he's following you... Iris, who are you to him?"

I look at my dad, then back to Ben.

"He's the one who took me," I say. "Eighteen years ago..."

Ben freezes, looking at me, as if trying to reconcile the history he's been told versus the truth we've laid out in front of him.

"The Night of Vanishing Children," he breathes. "December twenty-second, twenty-one forty-one?"

I nod.

"My god," Ben whispers, stepping back against the counter. "They said all the children were dead. Every report, every inquiry... They said you were all gone." He looks at me with a mixture of awe and terror. "How are you even alive?"

I don't answer. Because looking at the scars on my arms, I know the answer isn't luck.

"This changes everything," Ben says, already pacing. "I've been circling an angle for months trying to find a crack in the narrative, but this..." He stops, gripping the edge of the counter. "Shit, I can't run anything without UFN verification. That's always where it always dies. Horizon media policy."

"We can't involve UFN," I say, panic rising in my chest. "They tracked us across Chicago. They're the ones hunting me down."

Ben shakes his head. "Don't worry, I know a couple of UFN investigators," he says, lowering his voice. "They're covert global ops. Not local, not crimes division." Ben hesitates, choosing his words. "They operate higher up, in the shadows. They might actually help."

I look between my Dad, Lena, and Cal. "Can you guarantee our safety?"

"I've done it before," Ben says. "Whistleblower from a capital management firm. Massive insider trading. Never ran the story, but they put him into protection."

I take a breath, weighing the risk.

"Okay," I say. "I'll do it."

Ben's expression firms. "Good, once I'm at the studio, I'll place the call."

He sets his empty mug in the sink, opens a flush panel in the wall, and pulls out a backpack.

"I've got to head in," he says, slinging it over his shoulder, shifting back into his charismatic personality. "I'll be in touch."

The door closes behind him with a soft latch. Silence settles over the room, heavy with the decision I just made.

CHAPTER 11

Holding Pattern

In Ben's apartment, Lena slips easily into host mode, guiding us as if she's done this a hundred times before.

"Come on, Uncle Isaac," she says gently, pulling my dad up from the chair. "You need rest." She steers him toward one of the guest rooms, her hand steady at his elbow.

A minute later, Lena returns to the main room. "There are more guest rooms down the hall," she adds, pointing toward the corridor near the entrance. "Ben always keeps them stocked with fresh linens."

"Thanks," I say quietly.

Cal and I move into the living area and sink into the couch, exhaustion finally catching up with us.

"As for me," Lena says with a tired grin, already turning away, "I'm taking a long, warm bath and pretending yesterday never happened."

She disappears down the hall.

Cal and I look at each other, relieved to have a moment of silence.

"How are you holding up?" he asks softly.

"I'm okay," I shrug, though my words feel thin. "Just still shaken." My thoughts drift back to Elias, to the way the room felt when he spoke. "I felt completely disconnected from myself."

Cal picks up on my unease. "We're here now, though," he says, glancing around the room. "Somewhere safe." His voice lowers. "Out of reach."

I hesitate, finally voicing what's been haunting the back of my mind. "There's more, something I didn't tell you earlier. The augmentations the security scan flagged."

Cal straightens immediately, concern sharpening his expression.

"They're only the beginning," I say. "Elias, he has some level of control over me. Triggered states, some sort of psychosis unlocked by his command." I try to repeat the phrase he used, but my mind recoils, the words dissolving before I can finish them.

I press my fingers into the couch, grounding myself. "There's something always there now, a presence. When he showed me my record, it said I had a Quantum Neural Interface."

Cal's gaze locks onto me. I see recognition flicker behind his eyes, followed by something close to fear.

"Iris," he says quietly. "I've heard rumors about that. Not officially. Just, back-channel chatter."

He reaches out, hesitates, then gently touches my shoulder, feeling along the tender interface breaking the skin.

"That explains the hardware," he mutters, forcing a thin smile that doesn't quite land. "From what I've seen, that tech doesn't belong to this era."

He leans back, thinking.

"The original concepts go all the way back to the early twenty-first century. Experimental, almost military-adjacent. Some of it was tied to the old ISS programs and resurfaced during the war. "None of it was supposed to survive pre-commercial testing."

I look at him, my chest tightening.

"Then why do I have it?" I ask.

"And why does it feel like it's only just waking up now?"

Cal looks at me sharply and shrugs. "Tech like that," he says, "militarized and older than both of us, only ever gets unearthed during moments of crisis."

I nod slowly. In my gut, I know it's tied to my abduction. Whatever was done to me back then wasn't isolated. It was preparation. The full ramifications still sit just beyond what either of us can see.

"Cal," I say, meeting his eyes. His presence is steady, grounding. "We'll find the answers. They're out there somewhere."

He exhales, leaning back into the couch.

Time passes quietly as we sit above the city, suspended among the clouds. Eventually, he starts to talk.

He tells me about his childhood, turbulent and unsteady. His teenage years were marked by loss and anger. His father died when Cal was young, killed in an accident at the Sydney ports where he worked. After that, everything shifted.

His mother was a primary school teacher, endlessly patient with other people's children. But at home, the grief hollowed her out. She raised classrooms during the day, yet struggled to offer the same emotional safety to her own son and daughter.

Cal doesn't dramatize it. He doesn't need to.

I listen, understanding in the quiet spaces between his words.

"My sister, Maeve," he says softly. "She was my anchor. More of a mother to me than our own ever managed to be."

Cal pulls out his phone and scrolls, stopping on an old photo. He's younger there, still lanky, standing almost shoulder to shoulder with his sister. Maeve's arm is slung protectively around him, her smile confident, unshakeable.

"When Maeve turned twenty-six, she moved to Chicago for her residency," he says.

"She always claimed the opportunities were better out here.

Closer to Nova's Vancouver headquarters and core research facilities." Cal pauses.

"But really, she was escaping the mind games. The weight of living with our mom." His expression tightens, irritation flickering across his face.

"I was angry at her at first. Felt abandoned," he admits. "But after three years alone with Mom, I understood. Some people don't leave because they want to. They leave because they have to." He exhales slowly.

"I followed her to Chicago when I turned eighteen. University was never really my path."

He scrolls again and turns the phone toward me. A photo of his childhood bedroom fills the screen. A cramped desk buried beneath half-disassembled computers, tangled cables, open circuit boards, and networking gear stacked wherever it would fit.

"I was always tinkering," he says. "Programming systems, breaking things apart, seeing how far I could push them."

Cal smiles faintly.

"I went into the tech trades. Eventually landed a job with big old Horizon," he jokes. "Now I travel between megaregions, servicing the infrastructure that keeps the world running."

There's pride there, ownership in his words. But then it fades.

"Sometimes I wonder," he says quietly. "If all of this. The reliance on continuous connection." Cal pauses, weighing whether what comes next crosses a line. "If the surveillance that comes with it is just too much."

I sit there in his uncertainty with him, for a moment before answering.

"I think it's trying to hold the promise of something greater," I say carefully. "I just don't know if this is what the world is meant to look like forever."

Cal nods, as if not knowing is a good enough answer.

We sink deeper into the couch, exhaustion finally catching up with us. Time slips by unnoticed until the low murmur of the television pulls me back to the surface.

One of the glass windows has transformed into a massive display, scaled for newsrooms and executive suites. A movie plays across it, light flickering softly through the room.

I roll onto my side and see my dad sitting beside me, more present now, steadier.

"Iris," he says gently. "You've been out for a bit."

I glance toward the windows. The sun has nearly disappeared, deep purples and blues bleeding into the sky as night settles over the city.

"Lena and Ben should be back soon," he continues. "Sounds like he made some progress with UFN."

I follow his gaze to the other side of the couch. Cal is still asleep beside me, a blanket draped carefully over him. My dad watches him for a moment, then looks back at me with quiet warmth.

"He's a good man," he says. "I've never seen anyone aside from your mother give so much to people they barely know."

I smile faintly. He's right.

Not long after, the door opens. Ben steps in, Lena close behind him, arms full of pizza boxes and takeout bags. They set everything down, quickly turning the dining table between the kitchen and living area into a makeshift restaurant beneath the soft glow of the spherical chandelier.

"Iris," Ben calls, glancing over as he arranges plates. "I reached out and connected with UFN special ops."

My chest tightens, awaiting his words.

"They were vetted by my previous contact," he adds. "They are going to stop by tomorrow morning."

"Okay," I say, my voice steady despite the uncertainty swirling underneath. "I'll be ready."

"They think they can help," Ben says carefully. "Didn't offer many details on how."

Lena finishes setting out the food. "Alright," she announces. "Everyone, eat."

I gently nudge Cal awake, and soon we're all gathered around the table. The evening moves quickly after that, conversation flowing easily, laughter surfacing where it can. Soft music hums through the room. As the night stretches on, fatigue settles in again.

My dad heads to his room first. Ben and Lena follow soon after.

"Don't stay up too late, you two," Lena says teasingly as she disappears down the hall.

Cal and I remain at the table for a moment, the apartment quiet now except for the music and the distant hum of the city. The lights dim automatically, bathing the room in a warm glow.

We turn our chairs toward the windows.

Outside, tower lights blink against the dark. AVs and distant jets trace silent paths through the sky. Far below, the streets are nearly empty. Only a few cars and late-night pedestrians are finding their way home.

"I'm glad we made it here," Cal says quietly.

"Me too," I reply.

"What you did, getting us to New York," I add. "It means more than you know."

A gentle tension settles between us, unspoken but present. The warm light softens his features, strong and kind all at once.

He reaches for my hand.

I don't pull away.

CHAPTER 12

Carbon And Bone

That night, I settle in beside Lena in her room. Cal's hand still tingles in mine, the feeling lingering longer than it should.

I reach for the glass of water on the nightstand and pull the pill bottle Cal gave me from my pocket.

I hope Maeve is right about this.

I do not know if I am ready for another dose of Paxim. But tonight feels like the last chance I have to learn more about what happened to me, without others shaping my own truth.

I place the unassuming capsules in my mouth and swallow them down with room-temperature water. Anxiety settles in immediately. Is Maeve right? Will I keep reliving the night of my abduction? Or will I uncover new memories, reimagined as dreams?

Uncertain of what waits in the dark, I pull back the covers and ease into the bed. Lena whistles softly in her sleep beside me. The sound is faint, almost instinctive. My head hits the pillow, and it does not take long before sleep locks me in.

As deep sleep gives way to REM, I feel separated from my body. Like I am standing beside myself, watching my living flesh breathe. Awareness washes over me slowly, and the darkness of my inner thoughts fractures into something closer to the truth. A moment that exists long after I was taken.

I am standing inside a desolate, decaying apartment. I am older now.

The scale of the single-room home does not feel as daunting. My body aches, scarred and worn. I hold my arms out in front of me. Freshly sewn scars run the full length of them, still healing, the skin tight and angry.

My clothes are tactical, but thin from years of use, pushed beyond their limits. The apartment holds a small, unused kitchen and a bathroom covered in cracked tiles. The furnishings consist only of a solid metal desk, a built-in wardrobe that resembles a locker, and a narrow military-green bed, far from the warmth of my childhood home.

Through a thick armored window bolted into the wall, half-covered by metal shutters, I see the outside. Dust and toxic smog hang in the low afternoon light. A ruined city stretches across the horizon.

Towers reduced to skeletal frames. Facades shattered, melted away. The ground below is desert sand, scattered with cracked pavement and dead palm trees, everything blackened and charred by fire and sun.

I turn back toward the apartment's front door as voices echo outside. I pull the heavy latch. The door screeches and hisses as it retracts into the wall.

Beyond it, the space opens into a vast interior. Low ceilings give way to hundreds of levels rising upward, each lined with micro-apartments and abandoned storefronts.

At the top, just beyond eyesight, a glass canopy opens to a yellowing sky. Below, in the central courtyard, tables and seating areas sit in wide rings across the floor. Dozens of others stand and sit throughout the common area.

They are all around my age. Barely adults, and yet never children. Each one is a representation of their home region, a different background. Broad in diversity, captives of shared experiences, all gathered into one place.

I notice a girl sitting alone along the outer perimeter, separated from the others. Her features are familiar, a young friend I sense holds more memories, though her presence feels distant.

I start toward her. But strong hands grab my shoulders, holding me still.

Before I hear his voice, the scent of spearmint hits me. My body freezes, my mind and pulse racing.

"Iris." He says, forcibly turning me around.

Elias stands before me, younger here, ambition still sharp in his face. But his eyes are the same, grey, dark, lifeless, and watching.

"It is time," he says, lifting my forearm. His fingers trace the scars, still tender. I flinch, and he does not pull away.

"A marvel of bioengineering," he says quietly. "All that strength hidden beneath the skin."

He releases my arm and guides me toward the center of the courtyard.

The voices quickly lower as we step forward. Eyes follow us. Whispers ripple and fade amongst the crowd.

"Children," Elias calls out, his voice cutting through the silence. "Today, you will see what awaits many of you."

He grips my hand, his palm ice cold.

"Iris is proof of our mission," he continues. "To push the body beyond its mortal form. To become stronger, everlasting, and capable of conquering the systems that govern this world."

He lifts my arm into the air with his. I feel his false sense of triumph.

Faces in the crowd sharpen into recognition. Two young men stand together, concern is etched across their faces.

Another boy lingers partially hidden, his profile painfully similar to the lifeless body I saw on the lab's operating table.

Directly in front of me stands Julien, her blonde hair pulled back. Her posture is rigid, a flicker of envy crossing her face.

"Now," Elias says, turning to the others. "We need a baseline."

He scans the crowd for his victim. No one raises their hand. The air in the room is heavy with the fear of being chosen.

"Who is willing to test the limits of their own biology?"

Silence answers him.

"You," he says, pointing to the girl still seated against the wall.

The others step back, leaving her exposed.

"Come," Elias says. "Participation is never optional."

The girl nods and stands. Her shoulders are slumped as she moves through the crowd. Dark hair falls across her face. When she reaches us, her eyes lift in terror and lock onto mine.

"Good," Elias says. "Anya will be our subject. Take your positions."

The crowd parts, forming a wide perimeter. We move to opposite sides of the inner circle.

My body shifts into a fighting stance without conscious thought.

Elias raises a hand. He doesn't count down.

"The fault is not within us," he states. The words act like an activation key.

"It is corrected," the room whispers in response, a conditioned reflex.

Something inside me tightens as the inhibitor breaks.

Anya lunges forward, drawing a knife from her holster.

As she charges, time slows. Holographic projections bloom across my vision, mapping her possible movements. Every outcome favors her, except one.

Pain surges beneath my skin as something activates.

The world snaps back into motion. My vision locks onto her weakness.

I drop low, my movements hyper-scaling as I barely avoid the wrath of her blade. My hand clamps around her leg.

I apply too much force.

Bone cracks beneath my grip. I pull hard. She loses her balance, the knife slipping from her hand. I slam her into the concrete floor.

Her scream echoes against the sudden, suffocating silence of the room. No one cheers. The others just watch, frozen, witnessing a violence they know is waiting for them next.

Footsteps approach, calm and measured. Elias stops beside us, looking down at Anya, then at me. He doesn't smile. He studies the damage with the detachment of a technician, verifying a result.

He steps closer, invading the space between us. His hand reaches out, cold fingers brushing a stray hair from my forehead. A gentle, terrifying gesture of pride.

"Exceptional," he says softly. "Iris, this is why I chose you." Elias leans down, his eyes locking onto mine. "You are becoming exactly who I knew you could be."

My vision blurs. When it clears, the moment fractures. Anya is curled on the ground, crying out in pain.

The fight drains from me instantly.

I kneel beside her, reaching out, trying to calm her.

"Leave her," Elias commands, his voice losing its warmth. "She needs to grow stronger."

Guards standing by grab my arms and pull me away. Med-techs secure Anya to a stretcher and carry her through a set of reinforced doors.

I stare at Elias, disbelief burning in my chest. Anger surges, but my body will not move.

A block settles over my thoughts, preventing me from seeing him as a threat.

He pulls a device from his pocket and taps the screen.

"You are perfectly tuned," he says, sliding the device back into his coat. "Now we work on obedience."

The world fades. Darkness closes in, and the memory dissolves into the void.

I continue sleeping, but the weight of it lingers. Carbon beneath skin, bone made irrelevant. Immense strength, given without choice.

A nightmare pressed against the edge of my truth.

CHAPTER 13

Descent Into Ruins

Morning comes quietly, releasing me from the night.

I wake beside Lena, the blankets twisted around her as she sleeps on her side. The sheets below me are damp with sweat, wrinkled by restless sleep. She doesn't stir when I slip free, so I take the chance to get ready for the day.

The attached bathroom feels like an extension of the tower itself. Fluted marble walls curve into panels of dark green tiles, echoing the building's exterior.

The sink is carved into a single slab of stone, heavy and deliberate. The shower stretches upward, framed in warm brass.

I step beneath the rainfall, letting hot water and steam wash over me. The soap is rich, the scent unfamiliar but comforting. For a moment, I let myself feel clean again.

When I return to the bedroom, Lena is already up. The bed is neatly made. On my side, a stack of folded clothes waits, arranged with care. A small stationery card rests on top.

Got these for you.
A little touch of your Mom and Me.
Lena

As I unfold the outfit, the colors and patterns come to life. A silk blouse with buttons, beige with a pink geometric pattern embroidered along the lower hem. Dark navy denim stitched with bronze thread. Shoes designed to pass as formal, though built for movement. As I dress, the fabric settles lightly against my skin.

Before leaving the room, I lift my mother's jacket from the armchair and slip it on. It still smells faintly like vanilla.

Out in the main room, everyone has gathered around the kitchen island.

Coffee pours freely. Pastries are stacked high, indulgent, and warm.

"Good morning, hun," my dad says, looking rested and grounded.

"Good morning," I reply, joining them.

I take a seat beside Cal.

He shifts slightly, just enough to create space.

"So," Ben says, gently cutting through the morning calm. "The UFN investigators should be here shortly." He glances at me. "The advice I always give in situations like this is to trust your instincts. They may push for details. Try to steer you toward helping their own objectives."

I nod, unease settling in my chest. "Got it."

Moments later, a digital chime echoes through the apartment Ben rises and heads for the door.

Just outside, a man's voice carries clearly. "Agent Theo Grant and Amara Brooks."

"Nice to meet you both," Ben says as he opens the door. "I spoke with one of your colleagues yesterday. I appreciate you taking the time to come."

He steps aside, guiding them in.

The two agents pause in the center of the main room, taking us in with practiced calm. Grant is younger, composed, and almost polished.

Brooks is his opposite, dark-skinned, sharp-eyed, her presence immediate and impossible to ignore.

Her gaze finds me instantly.

"You must be Iris Vale," she says. "Agent Amara Brooks."

She steps forward and offers her hand. I take it, her grip firm and steady.

"We're glad to finally put a face to the name," Agent Grant adds. "When Ben contacted our team, we were already aware of your... condition."

A chill runs through me. "That's why you've been tracking me?" I ask carefully.

"Yes, in a manner of speaking," Brooks replies. "But we're not the only ones."

She hesitates, briefly weighing the room, then continues. "For decades, UFN intelligence has suspected Nova of operating beyond the terms of its charter. Unsanctioned medical experimentation. Unethical human trials."

Grant nods. "We also believe high-ranking Nova executives had ties to, or direct involvement with, the hundreds of children who vanished eighteen years ago."

The room goes still.

"Our investigations indicate many of the children from the Vanishing may still be alive," Agent Grant adds. "Hidden by Nova, enduring continued experimentation."

"We could never prove it," Brooks says, pulling a tablet from her coat and unfolding it. "Not from the outside."

Her eyes lift to meet mine. "All that changed when you escaped," she says softly. "You, and three others."

"So far," she continues, "you're the only one we've located. Our concern is that the others may be unstable or dangerous."

She holds the tablet out in front of me. Three surveillance images fill the screen, arranged in stark columns.

On the left, a young man stands rigid, both arms replaced entirely with augmented prosthetics, metal and polymer fused where flesh should be.

In the center, another man slumps against a retaining wall along the outskirts of the city, his hair singed, skin burned, eyes hollow with shock.

On the right, a young woman with dark hair that has fallen across her face. Her body is anchored inside an exoskeleton suit, its frame bolted directly into her spine and limbs, cables threading into her like veins. Something in me tightens. A recognition I can't explain.

My breath catches, it's Anya.

Agent Brooks notices the shift in my expression. "Horrifying," she says quietly, folding the tablet closed.

"We can't reveal more than this right now," Agent Grant adds. "But there are two individuals who want to speak with you." He hesitates, glancing at Brooks before continuing. "One is a woman currently in hiding. The other may be able to shed light on what happened to you."

I look back at my dad and Lena. Their faces are tense, but hopeful, caught between fear and possibility.

"You need to decide now," Grant says. "If you don't come with us, we'll have to move forward without your cooperation. And those plans may not guarantee your safety."

I weigh my options, though it hardly feels like there are any. Every path forward seems to lead deeper into the shadows, but the choice is still mine.

"Fine," I say at last. "I'll come with you."

Then I pause and turn to Cal.

"But can I bring someone with me?"

The agents exchange a glance, the silent calculus of protocol passing between them.

"You can," Brooks says carefully. "But whoever you bring can't go all the way."

I step over to Cal and take his hand. "Will you come with me?" I ask.

His eyes flicker with hesitation, the weight of the choice settling in. After a moment, he exhales.

"Okay," he says softly.

"Then we should go," Agent Grant says. "Our transport is waiting below."

I nod, and Cal stays close as the agents guide us toward the door.

Behind us, Lena calls out, her voice bright but strained.

"Good luck."

The door latches behind us.

We descend in silence, the elevator carrying us back down to the lobby. Morning light glistens through the glass as the doors open. Inside, a few residents pause and stare while the UFN agents usher us briskly toward the exit.

Outside, a large navy-blue SUV idles in the carport, UFN seals emblazoned along its sides. Agent Brooks opens the rear door and gestures us into the back seat. She follows, while Agent Grant takes the passenger seat up front.

The interior smells faintly of disinfectant. A black steel grate divides the rear cabin from the driver, solid and impersonal. On the dashboard, a single wide display shows a live map of the city. No destination is entered.

The vehicle pulls into traffic, its electric motors humming low and steady.

We accelerate toward an off-ramp that slopes sharply downward, leading beneath the upper layers of the city. Sunlight fades as we descend, replaced by tunnel lights that streak past the windows. The SUV weaves through traffic just below the top layer, banking through tight curves alongside delivery trucks and commuter vehicles.

Then we veer onto a narrow exit. Ahead, a massive metal garage door rolls upward. A projection spills across the pavement.

Caution: Enter Lift Slowly

The SUV glides inside. The door seals shut behind us with a heavy clang. The lift walls illuminate, light panels igniting along the steel interior. An automated voice fills the cabin. *"Please enter desired level."*

The driver taps the screen.

Level One

"Destination confirmed," the system replies.

A deep mechanical roar builds beneath us. The ground drops away.

The lift plunges downward, and the display on the dashboard begins ticking rapidly through numbers.

Level 900... 870... 820...

The subtle force lifts me in my seat. Through the reinforced glass walls, I watch the city peel past in layers. Each level grows darker, more compressed. The pristine whites and natural greenery of the upper city give way to artificial yellows and amber light. Sunlight becomes scarce, appearing only in distant slits far above.

At last, the descent slows. *"Arrived, Level One, East 46th."*

The lift doors part, and the SUV rolls out onto the street.

For several blocks, we pass through the city's oldest bones. Narrow roads entombed beneath towering structures, their foundations buried under almost a century of vertical expansion. Above us, entire layers of the city hang suspended, bustling in motion, sealing what lies below in a permanent, artificial twilight.

I realize we're no longer hiding. We're being taken somewhere that's never been seen.

The streetlights emit a tired buzz, some flickering from age, others dimmed by exhaustion. Sidewalks are littered with trash, and road surfaces cracked, and uneven from decades of neglect. We barely pass anyone down here, only the occasional displaced drifting by, sickly and withdrawn.

"It's a shame what became of this part of New York," Agent Grant says quietly. "In London, we grew up reading about the wonders of the UFN's shining metropolis." He pauses. "But never its history. The parts that were neglected and buried beneath the scale of progress."

Before long, the SUV slows at a security gate guarded by armed UFN officers. Ahead, a slender building looms, barely alive, only a few scattered floors glowing faintly within its frame. The upper windows are cracked, teal panes, yellowed by age and abandonment.

The gates roll back, revealing a long driveway that curves past a deserted fountain and a decaying façade. Around the perimeter, flags of former nations hang limp from rusted poles. Only a handful remain illuminated by weak spotlights below.

The SUV comes to a stop before the recessed entrance, stonework worn smooth by time. Agent Brooks steps out first. The air hits us immediately, thick with smog and waste. Cal coughs as he exits behind me.

We pass a group of guards stationed at the entrance, all wearing full respirator masks.

"Agent Brooks," one of them says through the filter, nodding.

She doesn't slow, ushering us forward into the building.

Inside, an old United Nations seal hangs on the far wall,

tarnished and cracked with age. Beneath it, a solid mahogany reception desk glows softly from a single monitor. An elderly woman sits behind it, hands folded patiently.

"Good morning, sweetheart," she says warmly to Agent Grant as he approaches.

"We're here to visit one of our special house guests," he replies lightly.

"Wonderful," she says, typing with practiced ease. "I'll call the elevator. First one on the right."

Agent Grant gestures us forward. "Come on."

We follow him across the lobby, Agent Brooks bringing up the rear. The building's age becomes unmistakable as we move deeper inside. Old televisions hang crookedly along the walls. Yellowed signage and framed photographs capture a world long past. The walls are decorated with former presidents, global leaders, and flags of sovereign bodies that no longer exist. Everything is preserved, untouched, and gathering dust.

One elevator stands waiting, its doors still open. Inside, the lighting is noticeably brighter. New and intentional. A sharp contrast to the decay surrounding it.

"Cal, you'll have to stay here," Agent Grant says, raising a hand.

Agent Brooks steps forward, resting her hand firmly on Cal's shoulder. I hesitate, then step into the elevator with Grant. He selects the panel.

Sublevel 17

The doors slide close, and Cal's face disappears from view.

The elevator begins its descent, the noise of the outside world fading with it. An eerie chime echoes softly as the doors finally open, deeper beneath the city.

The corridor beyond is nothing like the building above.

Walls of anodized metal diffuse clean white light calibrated to mimic the sun's circadian rhythm. Everything feels precise and controlled.

I follow Agent Grant down the corridor as we move further into the underground expanse. Our footsteps echo in the silence.

There are no voices here. Only the hum of voltage threading through the walls.

Agent Grant stops in front of a tall metal door. Above it, a screen glows softly.

Simulated Environment Active

He swipes his badge across the security panel beside the frame. A chime confirms access, and the massive doors hiss as they retract into the walls.

We step inside, Agent Grant leading the way.

The space beyond is unimaginable.

The room is cavernous, stretching so far in every direction that it feels infinite. Walls, ceiling, and floor dissolve into a living projection of a coastal shore. Tall grass ripples in the breeze. Waves crash faintly in the distance. I feel the wind move through my hair. The air carries the sharp scent of sea salt and seaweed.

Beneath my feet, sand gives way to weathered boardwalk pavers that lead toward a Cape-style home standing ahead of us.

Behind us, the doors close, then vanish, absorbed seamlessly into the illusion.

Seagulls cry overhead, their shadows crossing the ground as they glide above.

Agent Grant walks up to the front door and opens it.

"Eve," he calls. "Eve, we're here to see you."

"I'm in here," a woman's voice echoes from deeper inside the house.

As we step through the home, I trail my fingers along the walls, the furniture, the moldings, all solid and real. Every detail resists disbelief.

Photographs line the hallway walls. A woman and her son, captured year after year in the same sunlit room overlooking the ocean. In each image, he grows taller, older. Until eventually, he stands beside her as an adult.

My chest tightens as we turn the corner into the kitchen.

It looks like something pulled from another time. Warm wood, soft light, the quiet order of an old New England home. At the center, a woman sits alone at a round wooden table, a cup of tea cradled between her hands.

She looks up. "Iris," she says gently, meeting my eyes. "I wasn't sure this moment would ever come."

She extends her hand. I hesitate, my fingers hovering just short of hers.

Agent Grant steps forward. "Iris Vale," he says carefully. "Meet Eve Mercer."

CHAPTER 14

Cost of Inheritance

A knot forms in my stomach, tightening until it borders on pain. I stare at her outstretched hand, but I can't make myself take it.

Nausea rolls through me as the weight of where I am and who I'm standing with finally settles in.

"It's okay, honey," Eve says gently, lowering her hand as she notices my discomfort. She rises from her chair and pulls one out across from her. "Here, sit."

She pours another cup of tea from the softly whistling kettle and sets it in front of me, her movements practiced and calm.

"Easy now," she adds, instinctively maternal.

I wrap my hands around the cup and take a careful sip. The warmth spreads through my chest, grounding me just enough to breathe.

"I know my husband has committed terrible atrocities," Eve says quietly, resting her hands over my shoulders. "But I haven't been in contact with him in..." She pauses, choosing her words carefully. "Nearly as long as you've been gone from your parents."

"Okay," I manage to say, forcing my voice steady. "But why bring me here?"

She withdraws and sits back in her chair.

"This is my home," she says. "I've lived here for many years now. I don't leave, it's the only place I feel safe."

Her gaze shifts briefly to Agent Grant, then returns to me.

"I asked for you to come today because you were brought to my attention," she continues. "You've become something unexpected. An opening."

I tense up as her maternal warmth begins to erode. I'm not just a guest here, I'm her opportunity.

"You may be the key to dismantling what my husband has buried inside Nova," Eve says carefully. "To expose the systems he helped create. Ending the damage he's caused, and preventing a greater threat he now poses to the UFN."

The words hang heavy in the air. Before I can respond, the French doors to the sunroom open.

A young man steps inside.

He's tall, composed, and instantly familiar. His face echoes the photographs lining the hallway. The same bone structure. The same eyes.

"This is my son," Eve says softly. "Milo."

She gestures for him to sit. He takes the chair across from me without a word, his presence quiet but deliberate. Agent Grant joins us at the table, settling beside me.

"Milo is the reason you're here today," Eve continues. "For years, he's been my connection to the outside world. My safeguard. He's helped me gather what we need to hold Elias accountable."

I look between them, my thoughts racing. Eve turns slightly toward Milo, a subtle nod.

"Go on," she says.

Milo lifts his eyes to meet mine. And finally, he speaks.

"Iris," Milo says, his voice calm but weighted, "the lab breach wasn't uncontrolled chaos."

The air leaves the room as the words sink in.

"I assisted UFN special operatives in triggering the disruption," he continues. "The goal was to fracture Nova's containment systems long enough for those being held captive to escape."

I stare at him, stunned. "But how?" I ask. "And why so much damage?"

Images flash through my mind of the burned corridors. The cold bodies of lab technicians lying across the floor.

Milo's jaw tightens. "We didn't know how far it would cascade. We only knew the system had to break." He meets my eyes. "I did everything I could to make sure people like you had a window. A chance to reach safety."

"The others..." my voice trembles, "were you able to save them?"

Milo shakes his head. "You were the only one who made it this far," he says quietly. "The only one who escaped and chose to accept help."

I shake my head, trying to make sense of it. "So what? I was chosen?"

"No," Eve says firmly, cutting in. "Absolutely not."

She leans forward. "You weren't chosen, Iris. You were the only one who kept looking for answers."

She exhales, steadying herself. "The cognitive conditioning Nova used on all of you... It wasn't designed for freedom. It was designed for compliance. Stability just long enough to be useful."

I feel sick. "Then why am I the only one here?"

Milo hesitates, glancing at his mother before answering.

"The others went dark," he says. "One vanished into the city almost immediately. We believe another escaped into Nomad territory."

He swallows. "The third... her augmentations were pushed too far. Past the edge of consent. Past recovery."

"She killed the operative we sent to help her," Milo continues quietly.

My mind snaps back to the image of Anya on the tablet. Steel bolted to her flesh. The loading dock flashes in my mind. The crushed body, the blood, and oil streaked across the ground.

"She's the one in the exo-suit," I confirm. "Brooks showed me."

Milo doesn't look away. "Yes, she is exactly what happens when Nova is left unchecked."

"We know there are more like you out there, still captive." Milo pauses, leaning forward. "They're hidden in places we can't reach yet without raising flags."

Then he looks at me differently, carefully.

"And you," he says. "We placed a contingency. A controlled variable."

My chest tightens.

"We issued a false Horizon service request," he continues. "Subsurface anomaly scan. We needed someone nearby who wouldn't draw Nova's attention."

The room goes still.

I swallow. "Cal?" I ask softly.

The name hangs between us. Milo doesn't answer right away. And that silence tells me everything.

"Yes," Eve confirms quietly. "Cal Rowan."

Milo folds his hands together. "We believe he accompanied you here today."

Agent Grant nods once.

"The plan was clear," Milo continues. "We positioned him near the riverwalk that night. His social history showed strong indicators of intervention behavior. High empathy.

Low hesitation. We assumed that if he saw someone in danger, he'd help."

My jaw tightens.

"But when the explosions reached the upper lab levels," Milo says, "Nova security flooded the area faster than expected. Our surveillance picked up your jump into the river, and at that point, we had seconds to adjust."

He slides a tablet across the table.

Footage plays of me vaulting the railing. The river below swallowing me whole.

With a swipe, the screen changes to a message log with Cal. A single request, stark and undeniable.

Anonymous:
There will be a girl in the river.
Save her.

Another swipe. Footage plays of Cal's boat. My body breaking the surface. Me coughing water into the vessel.

Milo pulls the tablet back and folds it shut.

"We've been tracking you ever since," he says. "Intervening when we could. Redirecting when necessary. We never anticipated Elias staying this close. Or getting a hold of you and your family."

Milo pauses, his gaze shifting briefly toward Eve. "He's always been... faster than we expect."

Something clicks painfully into place.

Cal's hesitation. The half-truths. The way he never fully explained why he was there that night.

He didn't betray me. He just didn't know why he was asked to save me.

I steady myself, lifting my eyes to Eve and Milo.

They're watching me carefully now, like they know this is

the moment everything changes.

"So," I say, my voice firm despite the storm in my chest. "What's the plan?"

Eve leans forward, the warmth in her eyes replaced by a terrifying resolve.

"You kill Elias."

The words land clean, final.

A revolting clarity washes over me.

"My son helped you escape," she continues, her gaze unwavering. "Now you help me."

She leans forward, her voice low and certain.

"Freedom always has a cost, Iris. This is mine."

CHAPTER 15

Testimonial Fractures

I stop talking.

Across the table, Detective Calloway sits motionless, his attention fixed on me.

The interrogation room feels emptier now, stripped bare by everything I've laid out. The hum of the lights presses in.

He finally shifts, straightening in his chair. Metal screeches against the floor.

My arms are still restrained behind me. I flex my fingers, trying to force life back into them.

"So," Calloway says slowly, "what you're telling me is that a woman in witness protection and a handful of UFN special operatives convinced you to assassinate Elias Mercer."

His tone hardens.

"And you took that as an excuse for revenge," he continues. "To kill the man who abducted you."

I stare at him, irritation flashing hot and sharp.

"No," I snap. "His wife did."

Calloway blinks. "What?"

I draw a breath, steadying myself. "Why she killed Elias. Why hundreds of children were taken and experimented on."

My voice lowers, controlled now. "None of it started with me."

His expression shifts, uncertainty creeping in.
"It began with the Horizon Fault."
The room goes still.
I meet his gaze.
"And it wasn't an accident."

The record doesn't end here.

Continue Iris's journey through the Transition Age Trilogy.

Explore the world, receive future updates, and follow the story as it unfolds.

Learn more at: transitionagetrilogy.com
Follow the series: @transitionagetrilogy

About The Author

Tyler Corriveau grew up in the Greater Boston area with an enduring passion for science fiction across books, film, and television. From an early age, he was drawn to imagined worlds that reflected the complexities, fears, and possibilities of the real one. Storytelling became a way to explore systems, power, and identity through characters shaped by forces larger than themselves. That fascination with worldbuilding has remained central to his work.

As a creative professional, Tyler has witnessed the growing complexity and interconnection of the systems that govern modern life, from communication and social interaction to the technologies that quietly manage daily existence. The Transition Age Trilogy is the result of more than a decade of ideas shaped by those observations. Through science fiction, he explores how humanity adapts, resists, and redefines itself within systems designed to control it.

HORIZON FAULT

BOOK 02 | NEXT IN SERIES

Years before the events of Transition Age, a single city exposes the cracks beneath a carefully engineered future. In the aftermath of a catastrophic failure known as the Great Horizon Fault, the megaregion once called Seattle becomes a test case the world would rather forget.

Continue the story at:
transitionagetrilogy.com/books

www.ingramcontent.com/pod-product-compliance
Lightning Source LLC
Chambersburg PA
CBHW031143130726
47988CB00006B/2512